HIDE AND SPEAK

SECOND BOOK IN THE LABYRINTH TRILOGY

H L WELSH

the porridge press

Published by The Porridge Press.

ISBN: Paperback 978-1-9162418-4-8

Large print 978-1-9162418-6-2

www.hlwelsh.co.uk

CONTENTS

FOREWORD

This is the second book in the Flegg trilogy; here is a reminder of what happened in the first book, 'The Labyrinth at Flegg', in case it's been a while since you read it. There are spoilers here! If you haven't read 'The Labyrinth at Flegg' yet, you might prefer to read it first.

Flegg is a small town in the rural East of Scotland. In the town lie the ruins of a 12th century abbey, and a labyrinth has been built in those ruins. Unknown to nearly everyone, there is a stone in the labyrinth which acts as a communication portal between the everyday 21st century, and the 16th century – when the abbey was destroyed by the Reformers.

Morven is a 21st century girl, and twelve years old at the start of the first novel. She has survived a very traumatic childhood, and is being looked after by her great-aunt Ruth. However she has many fears to overcome as a result of past abuses, and often wonders why her own mother was so peculiarly unsuited to motherhood.

Back in the 16th century, a young French lad, Jean-Luc, is brought to **Flegg** by Brother Joseph, and works as a blacksmith in the abbey. When the monks are driven out by the Reformers, Brother Joseph arranges hiding places with some of the local landowners, and takes Jean-Luc with him to the nearby Glenmiglo estate. There, Jean-Luc meets and falls in love with Mairi, the steward's daughter.

However the hot-headed Jean-Luc is banished from Glenmiglo and sent back to France, leaving Mairi pregnant.

Morven and Jean-Luc discover each other through a misunderstanding in the labyrinth when, as part of a school project, Morven's class at school are burying time capsules. A tentative friendship begins.

CHAPTER ONE

Wrecked and befuddled, Mairi leant back in the hay. Lady Janet had collapsed to her knees on the barn floor, and was gazing at the blood-soaked straw, which someone would have to rake into a pile for mulching the kailyard. The Lady-turned-Midwife bit her lip, praying silently that she had done everything properly.

'How are you feeling now, Mairi?' she asked, for the nineteenth time, 'I hope your mother arrives soon.'

Mairi lifted the sheet and peeked down in horror at her mangled puss. Who would have believed it? Then she gazed at her new baby twins, the very manglers, wrapped and snuggled by her side. Soon it would be time to pick them up and explore – but not just yet. For the nineteenth time, she didn't know how to answer Lady Janet's question. She had never given birth before and had been completely unaware how dangerous the whole process could be. Not to mention, painful! It was something she'd never paid proper attention to, when her mother whispered the hopeless news of women or their babies – or sometimes both – dying in childbirth. At sixteen, Mairi had other interests, and thought she had plenty time to learn those secret things. But then she found she was wrong – to her mother's intense frustration.

A blurry memory wafted through Mairi's mind. 'Was that Jean-Luc earlier on? When I was in the middle of it all?'

Lady Janet glanced at the barn door. 'Jean-Luc?' she repeated, 'Well, er, how could it be? Isn't he still in France?'

The door swung open and Jess hove into view, come running to see whether her daughter was still alive. 'Mother!' cried Mairi, relieved at last.

'Are you all right?' Jess, experienced midwife and the birther of eight babies, five of whom had survived, swept her eyes over the scene. The bloody straw, the pooled afterbirth, her daughter's ashen face, and then the makeshift cradle.

'Two!' she gasped, 'Twins! I didn't see that coming! You'd think I'd have been able to tell...' and she leaned in with her fingers to inspect the babies' faces and appurtenances, and to listen for their breathing.

Lady Janet hovered, watching. 'I did my best, Jess, I hope I've done everything right, they both seem healthy at the moment...'

Tears started in Mairi's eyes, and she couldn't help her weakness. 'They're both fine, aren't they Lady Janet, you said they were fine?'

But the older women, having seen that Mairi had survived and that the two babies were breathing, needed to check everything all over again and Lady Janet needed to recount every detail of the births to Jess. 'Did I do all right?' she eventually asked, quite exhausted by her first ever midwifery adventure, and all too aware of the role reversal brought about by such a turn of events.

'Absolutely, Ma'am, I couldn't have done better myself,' said Jess, loyalty overcoming her anxieties. As far as she could see, everything was as it should be. 'Thank you so much for looking after her. I never expected her to come on so fast when I was heading up to the plum harvest.'

'Well you've always been such a help to me with mine, I thought maybe I could remember enough to help Mairi – but it's different, isn't it? Being on the other side of it.'

'Why don't you go off now and take a wee restorer? Beth and Peggy will be here soon, I'll get them to take away the bloody straw and tidy up. And Ma'am... thank you so much. I should have been here.' And finally, as Lady Janet took her grateful leave, Jess turned her attention to Mairi. 'Are you all right, my poppet? It looks like you managed just fine.'

'Oh, Mother,' Mairi wept, 'It was terrifying! Why didn't you stay?' But they both knew that in their position, the landlord's needs came first, and this included the harvesting of the first precious plums planted just last year by the rescued monks. In that moment, blue eyelids were fluttering open as one baby began to take stock of this unfamiliar world. Gently, Jess picked him up and examined him. His lips were pursing and sucking. She put him in Mairi's arms and, taking a breast, guided the little sucking mouth to its target.

'He's hungry!' said Jess. 'Look at him go!'

The strangeness of it! Mairi gasped a little as she felt herself being sucked out all over again. Then the other baby started whimpering. 'You will have to feed them both at once,' said Jess, 'or this other one will be howling in no time.

Here, turn him round, move his feet out the way... oh, it's a girl!' And, exhausted and shocked beyond herself, Mairi was lying back in the hay feeding two new arrivals from her own maiden breasts when her twin sisters arrived.

BETH AND PEGGY HAD BROUGHT A BUCKET OF WARM WATER FOR Mairi to get washed in, and some rags and baby things that her mother had put together, left over from five-year-old Davey as a babe. Jess gave them their instructions, then headed back down the hill to the cottage to get the fire on and some kale on the go. The girls cooried down in the hay, each holding one of Mairi's new babies. It wasn't their first experience of new babies – at fourteen, they both remembered the arrival of their younger brothers Will and Davey, now aged seven and five. Babies from their mother they took in their stride, but from their sister? Only two years older than them? This was a revelation. 'Look at all this blood! That's it! I'm never having babies!' They were full of questions and comments and observations, things they would never have dared ask their mother.

'And Mother says to put this salt in the water,' added Beth, producing a packet from her apron pocket. 'It's supposed to heal you ... are you cut or something?' But Mairi wouldn't let her look. 'Get off!' she protested, 'at least leave me with some things private!'

She loved her sisters' curiosity, but found herself entirely worn out. She washed her face and her top half with a warm wet rag, then rinsed it out and cautiously dabbed between her legs. Still a bit of fresh blood coming away, though much less than before. Her mother had said that everything was safe now; it was just a trickle and would stop soon. But when it was your own blood, it was worrying. She wiped gently, biting her lip at the horror of it. How stupid of her, never to have thought about all this before now! Suddenly everything felt fragile. She wondered if she would ever feel normal again. Meantime, here were two astonishing little babies, a boy and a girl produced from her own flesh! And no doubt put there by Jean-Luc, on that weird night of her father's death. Had he known what he was doing? It was almost unbelievable.

It was barely half a mile from the barn down to the cottage; Mairi had envisaged herself returning in triumph, proudly carrying her babies aloft. However, she felt so weak that she had to accept her sisters' help. Instead of the grand procession, they tottered along the path in single file: Beth at the front with one baby, Peggy next with the other, and Mairi limping along behind, trying to keep up as every step jostled her fragile innards.

Just in front of Mairi, Peggy was chattering excitedly. 'Guess what, Mairi!' She called over her shoulder, 'Mother has got places for Beth and me!'

'Both of us!' confirmed Beth, 'Not in the same house, obviously, but next door to each other.'

'Just about a mile apart,' added Peggy.

Mairi was dazed and couldn't understand what the girls were talking about. Places? What places? She was finding it difficult to keep her balance on shaky legs as she placed her footsteps down the stony path. 'What are you talking about?'

Beth stopped short, so that Peggy bumped into her, and they were both giggling and jostling each other while Mairi called out sharply, 'Be careful! Mind the babes!'

'Have you forgotten?' said Beth, her chestnut curls running wild down her back, 'We're going into service!'

They'd reached the stile that led over the hedge and into the back door of the cottage. Mairi sank onto the stile with relief. Thank goodness to sit down. She gazed wearily at her sisters. 'What do you mean, into service? Not *now*, surely? Mother has organised it?' As well as being weary, she was baffled. What on earth was happening to her world? But Beth and Peggy had hopped over the stile and rushed into the cottage to show the new babies their new home. Mairi sat for a moment, gazing up the hill at the fields, the cows, the distant orchard growing up the hillside. Then she summoned her strength, clambered over the stile and followed her sisters into the family home.

Jess was ladling soup into six bowls at the table. Three large portions, three small. She looked up as her daughters came straggling into the kitchen. Her face drooped now with sorrow and anxiety, her shoulders tensed. Not without tenderness, she put down the ladle and reached out to greet her new grandchildren. Her first grandchildren – and she certainly hadn't expected such a thing when young Davey was barely five years old. She felt Mairi's eyes on her as she took the twins in her arms. 'Two!' she murmured. 'How are you feeling now?' she asked as she nudged Mairi's arm with the crook of her elbow.

'I'm fine,' sobbed Mairi.

'Good Lordie, more twins... Shout to the boys, Beth,' she ordered, 'and we'll all have our soup. It's been a long day already.' Will and Davey came running in and greeted Mairi nonchalantly, casting a cautious glance at the two new babies as they grabbed their spoons and bowls. 'Sit up now!' said their mother, 'You'll get burnt.' So, they all settled round the table and ate their soup; onions, carrots and barley, all nourishing enough. Mairi began to feel a little more alive. When everyone had supped, Jess told Beth and Peggy to clear up then take the youngsters out for a while, and leave her alone with Mairi. And the babies.

'Tell me all about it,' her mother commanded, but Mairi didn't really have the vocabulary. It was all still so recent and her head was a jumble.

'Well,' she said, searching for facts not emotions, 'it took a while. It was sore. Lady Janet made me push, and then stop pushing, and then one big push and first we had this little one,' she indicated to the babe that Jess was nursing, 'and I thought, praise be that's all over, and then I got another shooting pain, and Lady Janet had a little bit of a prod at me, and said there was another one coming. So, I had to push and stop and push all over again, it was sorer than ever, and I don't know, maybe half an hour later? Out popped this one.' She laid a finger on the brow of the baby in her arms.

'Girl first?'

'Yes, and then the boy.'

Jess sighed, 'Two extra mouths to feed.'

Mairi drew in a sharp breath, 'I'll be feeding them,' she said, 'There won't be any extra food needed for a while.'

Jess sighed at her daughter's ignorance, 'You know nothing! How do you think you're going to keep your strength up to feed two hungry babies, if you don't eat plenty for yourself? And they won't be breastfeeding forever.'

'I'll manage... but... Are Beth and Peggy really going

away?' Mairi couldn't contain her anxiety any longer on this count.

Her mother sighed again, 'Over on the Nine Bells estate. That's for Peggy. And then just over the hill round by Earnhead, the factor's family needs an extra pair of hands. That's for Beth. I'm lucky to have got positions for them so close by.'

'But why?' cried Mairi, 'Why can't they stay here with us?'

'You knew this would be happening soon! Remember, we talked about it after your Father died!'

But Mairi's memory was groggy with the events of the last twenty-four hours, and she couldn't get past how much she would miss her sisters. 'Why now?' she cried, feebly.

'It's all very well for you, Missy, sitting there with your brand-new babies, thinking the world owes you a living! How on earth do you think I'm to make ends meet? Ever since your father died, it's been obvious that the twins would have to go into service – and it's not such an awful thing either. I liked it well enough as a youngster, once I got used to it, anyway. It was all about growing up. Why, you yourself would have gone into service at fourteen, don't you forget, if Lady Janet hadn't made such a fuss about keeping you here. I wonder if she looks back now and thinks that was a mistake?'

Mairi refused to cry, but her chin wobbled dangerously. One of her babies started a long, thin, keening, quickly followed by the other. It was as if they were absorbing her feelings, she thought, of loneliness and disappointment and fatigue. Jess cut into her thoughts, 'They're hungry,' she said, 'you'll have to feed them.'

'Again? Already?'

'Aye. You'll need to get used to it.'

Inexpertly, Mairi fumbled at her blouse and manoeuvred first one twin and then the other into position, trying to find the way her mother had shown her earlier on. Jess leaned down and made sure that the little mouths were latching firmly onto Mairi's breasts, and then that Mairi was comfortable. She brought a stool for her daughter to put her feet up on while she fed the babies.

'You might as well get comfortable, Sweetheart. You'll be spending quite a lot of time in that position for the next few days. I'm away to feed the hens while you get on with it.' And she clattered off into the yard.

Left to her own devices, Mairi allowed herself to be sucked at vigorously, while her tears fell. It wasn't exactly sore, having the babies latched onto her like this, but it was surprisingly strong and she wasn't sure if she liked it or not. What was wrong with her? She was never usually this feeble. Maybe it would all feel better tomorrow, after a good night's sleep. Her mother came back into the room, bearing a mug of a hot herbal brew. 'This will help you heal down below,' she said and then, a little more kindly, 'Don't fuss about things today, just get used to the babies. After you've had a few days' sleep and got them into a routine, it'll all be fine. They're looking healthy enough.'

'When will Beth and Peggy go away?' Mairi couldn't bear the idea of home without them. Of being stuck here with her mother in this anxious mood, without her sisters to chatter away the gloom, and do a bit of fetching and carrying for her till she caught up with herself.

'Sunday,' replied her mother, 'Three days hence.'

'Oh, Mother!' Mairi whimpered, 'So soon! How can you bear it?'

'Bear it? Bear what? It'll be good for them. Once they get used to it, they'll enjoy it. And it'll bring in a few pennies. We'll see them once a week, on their day off. They'll be well fed, and learn a thing or two. It's what young girls do around here – young girls from poor families anyway. It didn't do me any harm.' But there was a catch in Jess's voice and a vacant sadness in her eyes.

Mairi was silent for a while, brooding on life and its twists and turns. Then she brightened a little. 'But Mother,' she said, 'don't forget – Jean-Luc will be coming back!'

'Really?' said her mother, thinking that perhaps this wasn't the best time to tell her daughter that Jean-Luc had been seen scurrying away in the opposite direction earlier that very day.

'That's right!' said Mairi. 'And he will look after us all – he's so strong, he will do everything that Father used to do...'

'So where is he going to live?' asked Jess, stung and beginning to wonder what exactly her daughter's plans were.

'Well, here of course!' said Mairi, fully confident that this was an excellent plan. 'He's as strong as an ox! Sir Peter will be delighted to have a good strong man in the cottage again, and...'

'In this cottage? Don't be ridiculous!' snapped Jess, perhaps more firmly than she had intended. 'You think you can take your Father's place so easily? I'll have you know this cottage was in your Father's family for five generations! We are not just handing it over to the first fortune hunter who comes looking for an easy bed for the night. You should have thought twice before you lay with that young man my lady, and you might as well face up to it. He won't be the one to put bread on our table.'

'Fortune hunter? What kind of fortune have we got?'

'Barely enough to keep body and soul together, and that's the truth!'

Mairi was aghast. 'What do you want me to do, Mother?' she gasped. 'I know he'll be back – he promised! In fact,' and she racked her brains, 'I may be dreaming it, but I think he may already have come back. I thought he turned up earlier on today, when I was in the middle of having the first baby.'

Nothing else for it. Jess was going to have to tell her daughter the hard truth. 'Yes, he's been back,' she said, her voice thick with disgust, 'and Sir Peter gave him a flea in his ear and sent him away again. So, you will have to look else-where for your way out of this mess.'

Stunned, Mairi finished feeding her babies, cleaned up their dirt and limped down to the burn to rinse out the clouts in running water. Then she took the babies and herself off to bed as the sun slipped down the sky. She believed in Jean-Luc; she knew he would return. And in the morning, she would figure out a way to make things better. She gazed at her little babes sleeping beside her. They would have to have names soon. That was another job for tomorrow.

Exhausted, she fell asleep before the last scarlet ripples had faded from the top of the Strath, oblivious to the hushed giggles and packing noises made by Beth and Peggy as they began putting together their belongings for their Sunday departure.

CHAPTER TWO

Up the Strath to the west, brilliant blood orange streaked the sky; the reflections on the water were almost mirror-like, there being no wind to stir its glassy surface. It was the serene evening of a perfect harvest day.

Jean-Luc however did not even notice the sky. He hustled down the path to Flegg, stumbling away from the setting sun, his steps agitated and clumsy. What a contrast to the manner in which he had leapt up the hill, like a very gazelle, earlier in the day! He could not believe they had thrown him out so unceremoniously. He forged ever onwards, shame driving him. That Sir Peter should have sent him away so sternly! Sir Peter must have known that Mairi was bearing his child? However, it was news to Jean-Luc himself. If only Brother Joseph had been at home – and how ironic that the monk had headed for France just as Jean-Luc was returning.

He was a father! Really? He could hardly believe it. How on earth had that happened? His oldest brother André had recently become a father, to his parents' great joy. But André was a full five years older than him, and Jean-Luc certainly hadn't looked for this in his immediate future. It must have been that night in the hayshed. That wonderful night, when they had locked him up for his part in Hugh the steward's fall into the quarry, but Mairi had come visiting him, bringing her supper to share. He could never stop thinking about it, it was his most delicious memory. But he had never considered that a baby might be the result. So easily? He smiled a little and decided it was splendid news. For him, at any rate.

Mairi would soon win his father over. And his mother too, although that might take a little longer. He could imagine how they would croon over a grandchild. Was his room back home big enough? Would Thibault be willing to move out? They would all shuffle up, make room, he was sure Mairi would be happy.

It crossed Jean-Luc's mind that perhaps Mairi would find it hard to leave her mother and other family members behind; vaguely he remembered there were younger brothers and sisters. What if she couldn't face that separation? That was something to think about. Would he need to go back to France alone? And live as if he didn't have a child over the sea in Scotland? He frowned.

Normally Jean-Luc would have called in at the forge on his way down through Flegg, for a bit of a blether with Arthur the blacksmith, and to catch up with the village news. On this occasion, however, he felt too conflicted to do so, not ready to share the momentous news. If only he had known that Mairi was pregnant! It must have been awkward for her, he realised, carrying his baby all those months without him there to support her. People in the village would have reacted in different ways, but Jean-Luc was fairly sure that eyebrows would have been raised, and she may have had to put up with spiteful comments from some quarters. How ashamed he felt, to have left her in that state and not been able to do anything about it. If only he had known! He would have come straight back – although then Sir Peter would still have thrown him out. What on earth was he to do?

His steps slowed down and bent towards the Abbey, in its sorry deserted state. He would take shelter there, crouching where nobody could see him, and figure out what to do next. There were fat juicy plums on the trees, and a few under-ripe apples. It reminded him he hadn't eaten all day, and he feasted hungrily on the fruit, swatting away a determined wasp. Away downriver he could just see the wake of the last ferry of the day, headed for either St Andrews or Dundee. Whatever he decided, it would probably have to wait till tomorrow. Or else he could walk.

A little calmer now, he considered his options. Maybe he could try Sir Peter again the next day. Perhaps with a little time to think it over, the landowner would see things differently? Somehow, however, Jean-Luc doubted it. It would be so good to see Mairi though.

His friend the blacksmith would surely be sympathetic to his situation? Yes, he would visit Arthur tonight, and after that he would be in a better position to decide what to do. Tomorrow, he could get the ferry to St Andrews, and head right back to France. Or he could stay around for a while... see how things might fall into place.

With its final magnificent adieu, the setting sun gazed

straight into the outline of the bear on the hill above the Abbey. Jean-Luc noticed the bear now, as if for the first time. He had forgotten how magnificent it was! He felt a new fondness for the beast, noticing how similar in stature it was to his own solid bulk. He might only be 15 years old, and perhaps hadn't even finished growing, but he had his feet well planted on the earth.

Did his baby have his feet? Sometimes that happened, he seemed to remember from his mother's chatter. He was curious to know.

Emptying his pockets for safe keeping, he left a little pouch with a few coins under that loose stone in the labyrinth - the stone where he had corresponded with the mysterious young Martin-Morven. No little notes on this occasion, he noticed. He added his pocketknife to the hole in the ground, and then thought better of it, sliding it back in place under his robe; you never knew when you might need a weapon. A scatter of tiny metal letters showered into the hole along with the pouch, unnoticed. He quickly covered the hole over with the stone, and set off up the hill to the village, to visit the blacksmith and to figure out a plan.

CHAPTER THREE

Meantime, nearly 500 years later, a twelve year-old girl and two older women strolled along the harbour front in Arbroath – maybe twenty miles to the North of the town of Flegg. The girl was called Morven – also known as Martin, but to only one other person throughout the centuries. Her aunt was called Ruth and they both addressed the other person they were visiting as Aunt Linda.

This was the first time Morven had met this distant relative, whom her Aunt Ruth had discovered in the process of working on their family tree. 'What is she to me again?' she had pestered Ruth, as they sat on the train. Ruth folded up her magazine and put it in her handbag, the train just leaving Dundee; she reckoned on another twenty minutes in the train at most. 'Just what I told you before,' she said, 'She is my aunt – my mother's older sister. That makes her your granny's auntie.'

Morven was concentrating, 'So, your sister was my granny?'

'Uh huh.'

'Alison? I just about remember her.'

'You were four when she died. That's right, Alison was my older sister.'

'Did she know my Mum? Not Alison I mean, her auntie, Linda. Her that we're going to see today.'

Ruth paused, 'I think she must have done, although I can't really remember. We can ask later on if you like.'

As the train trundled North, Ruth and Morven fell silent again, each occupied with their thoughts. It was a mystery to them both, how Morven's mother Aileen had turned out to be so disastrously ill-equipped for parenthood. Maybe Linda would be able to shed some light on this, and perhaps also to help Ruth figure out the further reaches of the family tree. 'It might be a bit heavy to go into all this on our first visit,' Ruth mentioned to Morven, 'maybe we should get to know her a little bit before we give her the whole story – about Aileen, and all that.'

Morven nodded silently, her eyes darkening. It was all so recent, still so painful. 'Do you think Linda will be... normal?' she pondered, visions of drug dens swimming in her mind.

'Well – who knows whether there's anyone normal in our family!' Ruth joked. 'She sounds normal enough in her emails though.'

'What shall I call her?'

'I think we should both call her Aunt Linda,' said Ruth, 'and if she doesn't like that, I'm sure she'll tell us.'

'Okay.'

Linda was waiting for them at the station. She was a thin, slight women with fading red hair, tricked out with a few sky-blue highlights. She wore a short navy duffel coat with wooden toggles, a long, multi-coloured tie-dyed scarf, and she walked with a stick. Ruth remembered the India experiences. Her mother would never have dressed like that, but then her mother had never left Flegg. She was intrigued by Linda, but also a bit anxious about raking up the past. There was a lot of shame on the edges of Ruth's childhood memories, associated with her sister Alison and mitigated by her mother's protection. Her memories of Linda were vague, and she wasn't sure how Linda fitted into the family story. Meeting her was perhaps risky, for both her and Morven, but surely better to face up to what there was to know?

She and Morven approached the waiting Linda with cautious smiles. Linda was smiling too, and embraced them both with a degree of warmth. 'It's good to see you,' she murmured into the collar of Ruth's jacket, 'I am glad you got in touch, Ruth. It's been such a long time. Thank you for coming.'

They went for a walk round the harbour, spying out the sturdy working fishing boats along one edge, with the little pleasure crafts bobbing up and down opposite. They read the inscriptions on the memorial cairns for fishermen drowned at sea. They bought some fat golden fishy things called Smokies and walked back to Ruth's home with them. She lived in a little flat above a chandler's shop near the harbour; her home was full of amazing objects and pictures and books, and Morven couldn't wait to explore it. At Aunt Linda's invitation, she searched for forks and plates and kitchen roll, and set them out on the kitchen table. Her aunt was putting together a great big salad using the Smokies she'd just bought, adding in potatoes which, she explained, had been handed in to her that morning by a friend who had grown them in his allotment. There was also a big bowl of lettuce and cucumber and tomatoes and spring onions, all tossed together with a lemony dressing, and a fat brown cob of bread, fresh from the bakers next door. Linda laid a bread knife beside the loaf, and a dish of yellow butter. There was a jam jar on the table with a bunch of flowers which looked as if they had been picked off the roadside verge, and another jam jar with a handwritten label saying 'Carnoustie Blueberry July 18'. It was all very colourful and welcoming. Morven hoped, with careful optimism, that this Aunt Linda was going to be a good thing in her life. But it was too soon to tell.

'What exactly is this fishy stuff?' she addressed her new aunt.

'Fishy stuff? I'll have you know these are best North Sea haddock, smoked over a hardwood fire,' laughed Linda, 'Have you never seen them before? Or tasted them?' Morven shook her head. 'You're in for a treat then!' said Linda, 'They just came out of the sea yesterday morning. Arbroath is a great wee town. Remember the harbour had a big shed on one side? That's where they hold the fish market. Leave the dishes and we'll go for a walk and I'll show you round.'

So off they went, on a stroll around the town and to Morven's surprise, they came across the ruins of an enormous Abbey. 'Look!' she said, 'just like Flegg! Bigger, though,' she acknowledged.

'I think it was the same order of monks who founded the abbey here,' said Linda, 'From France. It's twelfth century.

And of course, there was the famous declaration of Arbroath, which was signed here by Robert the Bruce and all the other landowners. It's a very historic place you know.' Aunt Linda seemed to be proud of her home town - or the town she had adopted as home. Morven stored that in her mind for later. Why had she left Flegg? Then her eye was caught by a colourful gathering of young people, spread out on the grass behind the Abbey with sketchbooks and pencils. 'Look at them!' she exclaimed. 'What are they doing?'

'Oh, they'll be art students up from Dundee or Glasgow,' replied Aunt Linda, 'They come here every summer. This will be the last lot, I think, before the weather gets too cold for outdoor sketching.'

'Art students?' queried Morven, 'What does that mean?'

'It's youngsters who go off to study art after they leave school,' replied Ruth, 'instead of going to study other things at college or university, if they are good at art they might get into art school and concentrate on drawing and painting and other arty things, like I suppose, pottery or sculpture or something like that.'

'You mean you can just do art and nothing else?' breathed Morven in delight. Her two aunts nodded. 'That's what I'm going to be then,' said Morven firmly, 'I'm going to be an art student when I grow up.'

'Great idea,' said Aunt Linda, 'I'll help you – if that's okay?' she added, seeing the caution on Morven's face.

'Did you go to Art School, Aunt Linda?'

'No. I couldn't wait to leave school, didn't have the qualifications. And I wanted to see the world.'

'You need qualifications?' Morven's face fell. That was a different story.

'Not to be an artist. Just if you want to do it the academic way.' Ruth caught Linda's eye. 'We can talk about it another time.'

An ice cream van was parked nearby. 'Let's get a cone,' said Aunt Ruth, 'my treat.' She stood in the queue and contemplated the idea of Morven as an art student. It would make sense. Morven definitely had an artistic talent. If she could settle down enough to get a few qualifications at school, she might just manage to get into art school. Ruth had no experience of higher education; it hadn't visited her family. 'Three 99s, please,' she said to the woman behind the counter when it came to her turn. Fiddling for her purse, she reflected that she could barely afford to pay for the ice creams, never mind fund her great-niece through art school.

Later that night, Aunt Linda saw them off at the station, and as they were boarding, she handed Morven a little brown suede pouch and told her to open it on the train. 'It's just something I think you'll like, that belonged to your granny,' she said, 'and a sweetie for the journey. See you soon!' Morven and Ruth waved to Aunt Linda from the train window till the train swung south towards Dundee.

Ruth and Morven got themselves seats at a table, and settled down. 'Well, that went well!' said Ruth, recognising that she trusted Linda. 'I liked her. Did you Morven?'

'Yeah it was great,' muttered Morven, opening the little leather pouch which her new Aunt Linda had given her. 'What do you think this is?' First of all, she found a packet of Polo mints, and then a tube of fruit gums, and then a chocolate fish, wrapped in shiny gold paper.

'A chocolate fish!' she exclaimed, 'I've never seen one of them before. It must be another Arbroath speciality.' But the pouch wasn't empty yet. There were some tiny objects clinking at the bottom, and she poked in but couldn't quite reach with her fingers. She tipped the little pouch into the palm of her hand, and out poured a little pile of metal printing press letters. She gaped in amazement.

'What are those?' asked Ruth.

'It's the little letters like I found before!' said Morven, 'Remember I found the M in the labyrinth?' Ruth couldn't remember this at all, actually, but she just nodded. 'What are they for?'

Morven said nothing. She was holding the letters carefully between her two palms allowing them to warm up and warm up, until yes! They started vibrating. Just like the M she had before. She gazed at Aunt Ruth, who was extremely puzzled by all of this. 'What are they?' she asked again, but Morven just shushed her. She closed her eyes and saw again, flickering faintly at first and then bright and clear – the beautiful girl with the auburn hair, serene and smiling as ever. But this time, in each arm, she carried a tiny baby. 'Are they really babies?' Morven strained to make out the detail. Maybe they were little piglets, or hamsters, or some other kind of small animal like that? Maybe this M was also an animal lover. But the vision was fading, despite Morven's vigorous rubbing of the letters between her palms.

Aunt Ruth was speaking, interrupting the moment, 'Morven – what's going on?' she was asking, a little alarmed. Morven opened her eyes. 'Nothing really,' she replied, remembering that her Aunt had gone ballistic at the mention of a Frenchman in the labyrinth. Of course, that was just after the unfortunate incident with the creep in the car park, and naturally, Aunt Ruth had no concept of time travel. Most adults didn't, Morven had found. Carefully, she shook the letters out onto the pouch lying on the table between them. Ruth picked one up and peered at it. 'These belonged to Alison?' she said, creasing her brow in puzzlement. 'I don't remember Alison having these. They look like they're from an old printing press or something.'

'Oh well,' said Morven, gathering the letters up and putting them back in the pouch. She drew the strings together. 'It's nice to have something that belonged to my granny. Did you tell her about the family tree?'

'Briefly.'

'And will she help?'

'Yes, I think so; she said something about laying old ghosts.'

'Ghosts?'

'Just a figure of speech.'

'Her sister's? My granny's?'

'I don't know. Not real ghosts. We're going to meet up again soon and talk some more.'

Morven opened the fruit gums. 'Tell me about art school again.'

Ruth's trusty old Micra was waiting for them in the station car park at Kinbuckie, but when they'd got themselves in and settled and Ruth turned the key, there was none of the usual cough and rumble. Tutting in irritation, Ruth tried again three times, gave it a rest for two minutes and tried again – still no joy. She Googled the garage in Flegg, but of course it was closed at this time of night. Peter, one of the mechanics there, she knew would do her a favour – but she didn't have his personal number. Eventually, after texting three different friends, she managed to get in touch with Peter who said he would come and collect them. Half an hour later he arrived. He had a quick look under the Micra's bonnet and said there was nothing he could do right away. Next day, they could come and tow it back, but in the meantime, the best he could offer was a lift back to Flegg for Ruth and Morven.

Ruth hesitated. She had hoped that Peter could get her car to go straight away, if he would just take the time. Maybe he'd been otherwise engaged; she'd heard rumours that he was seeing a woman from up the hill. To be fair, he'd come as soon as she asked him, which was well beyond the call of duty. On the other hand, she was anxious about the cost of a tow back to Flegg the following day, to say nothing of the eventual repair cost. 'Do you think it's fixable?' she asked nervously.

'Oh yeah,' said Peter, 'these old Nissans last forever. But you definitely need a new battery. And possibly also a starter motor.'

'A new battery and a starter motor? How much will that cost?'

But Peter was impatient to get on the road. 'I'll get you the price tomorrow,' he promised, 'but you could be talking three figures.'

There was no choice really; they couldn't just leave the Micra in the station car park. And meantime their cats would be prowling around waiting to be fed. So, Ruth and Morven climbed into Peter's truck and went rattling back to Flegg, enjoying a higher-up view of the surrounding fields than usual.

Ruth wondered whether she should enrol on a mechanics class at night school, not at all her cup of tea. Even the mechanics were getting younger these days, so there wouldn't even be an opportunity to meet some man – a fantasy she still nursed from time to time. She knew she couldn't afford to replace her car, and that the trade-in value of an eleven-year-old Micra would be virtually nil. So, If Peter couldn't fix it, it would need to be bus travel from now on. This was a bit depressing; it would cut down their options so much. All the little trips that she had planned for herself and Morven at the weekends and in school holidays would go by the wayside. Not for the first time, she wondered how she could raise some extra cash.

Since starting at High School, Morven had survived her own introduction to the bus service – having had to get used to the school bus to Kinbuckie. There were always some bullies on the back seat, who took great delight in calling out names, stealing schoolbags and tossing them overhead, and other delights like that. She was now in possession of a mobile phone which was a great adventure, and Ruth's 'Don't give out your number!' was advice she was trying to abide by - but it wasn't easy.

She stuck with her friends, mainly Jennifer and Kyle, for safety on the journeys to and from school. However, Morven resented the teasing, and being treated like an idiot; on more than one occasion she had squared up to the bullies and taken them on in verbal battle. Her ability to deliver a prolonged stream of fruity abuse had intrigued the bullies, who couldn't decide whether to swat her into oblivion, or recruit her as one of their own. So, the school journey was always quite challenging, and Jennifer and Kyle became quite anxious whilst trying to keep their friend out of trouble.

High school itself was mixed, two weeks into the new school year. As Morven had predicted, Jennifer had taken to it like a duck to water and quickly developed a whole wide circle of new friends - into which she tried to welcome Morven and Kyle. Morven hung around on the edge of that circle, not very skilled at making friends, and glad to have a place to stand in the playground at breaks and lunchtime. However, she hadn't found anybody apart from Jennifer and

Kyle to get to know and trust and she didn't feel part of that group. Kyle had settled in rather more cautiously; he was anxious about being seen as the stupid one in class so he clung to Morven for reassurance. Morven didn't understand his fear but tolerated him well enough. Though as Kyle got used to the new timetable, and got to working well with his learning support teacher, he became more confident. He discovered he wasn't the only one with dyslexia and became generally more relaxed. His friendships with other children in his support group developed, and he saw less of Morven during the day. Generally, it was only on the bus journeys to and from school – when Morven's behaviour sometimes frightened him – that the two of them met up.

Morven told herself that she didn't care about school, or the silly lessons, but the conversations she had had with Aunt Ruth about art school confused the picture. It seemed, to her puzzlement, that simply being good at drawing and painting weren't enough on their own to get you to art school. You also had to pass exams in things like English and Maths and various other subjects, like History or Geography or Science. Why? Those things wouldn't help her be an artist. History, geography, science – these were another world to Morven, and she couldn't see how she could ever pass exams in these subjects.

Wednesday afternoon was double art. This was the absolute highpoint of Morven's week, and the only reason why she didn't slip away at lunchtime and play truant. Her art teacher was Mrs Morrison who, as it turned out, had also been Ruth's art teacher at school twenty-five years previously. Ruth remembered Mrs Morrison, although probably Mrs Morrison didn't remember Ruth, who had no particular artistic abilities. On the third Wednesday afternoon of term, Mrs Morrison had laid out half a potato and a little carving tool on everybody's desk. They were to cut out shapes into the surface of potato halves, and then dip them in paint and print them onto paper. Morven was fascinated by this. She realised that the little letters found in the labyrinth were another version of the same thing – this explained why some of them were in reverse and would only read correctly once printed out.

Mrs Morrison asked them to make an abstract carving which could be used to print a repeat pattern on paper. The plan was to cut out a pattern and then stamp it in rows and columns all over an A3 sheet of paper, so that it looked like one big regular pattern. They could use different colours if they liked, but they had to use the same potato prints.

Morven didn't want to do abstract today. Normally she quite liked doing abstract things, but her mind was still very taken up with the vision she had had on the train of her great-great-great etcetera Grandmother M. So, she carved out an oval face in her potato, with big eyes and long flowing hair, billowing out behind. Mrs Morrison came round looking at the pupils' results at the point where they were being printed onto paper. Morven could hear her coming along the row making positive and approving statements to all the other pupils, and she readied herself for praise. But when Mrs Morrison came to her side, and looked at her work, she was silent for a while, till Morven looked up at her.

'It's not abstract, is it Morven?' she probed.

'Well, no, but I wanted to make this picture...' said Morven.

'Is this a picture of somebody you know?' asked Mrs Morrison.

'Well not exactly, but I've seen her in my – in my imagination.'

'Maybe you should have a shot at drawing people in real life, Morven,' said Mrs Morrison, 'Then you'll be able to learn how to capture a true likeness.'

'Don't you like my potato print?' asked Morven, her face falling.

'Well,' said Mrs Morrison, 'it's not that I don't like it, but look – it doesn't make a good pattern, does it? It doesn't fit the brief. And I would also say that it's not your best work. It looks like a cartoon, copied from some film or other. It's too perfect, just like people in cartoon characters, whose perfection is unrealistic.'

The other pupils in the class were listening in. Unknown to Morven, the other pupils in the class liked her drawings, and couldn't see what was wrong with being able to draw a brilliant picture of a cartoon character, just like the real thing. Mrs Morrison realised she was no longer having a private conversation with Morven, and also that Morven was struggling to understand her reaction. She addressed the class.

'When you find you have a talent,' she said, 'you need to work hard at it. Copying is all very well, but it doesn't take you as far as really trying to see things for yourself. A great artist is someone who looks straight at things and tries to represent them honestly, without the need to conform to popular ideas of beauty. Who is to say that, for example, Snow White's good looks are especially admirable? What a good artist needs to do, is be open to things just as they are, and to be honest in representing that on paper. Warts and all.

'Just keep on with your printing, please.' And Mrs Morrison resumed her walk around the class, commenting on everybody's work. It seemed to Morven that she was the only one in the class who had not been praised, and her eyes stung in humiliation.

The other pupils had quickly lost interest, but Morven was feeling very raw as she left class at the end of the lesson. Mrs Morrison stopped her on the way out. 'Morven,' she said, 'I'm sorry that became a bit public; I want you to know, you have a good talent, and I would like you to develop it as much as you can. If anybody else had carved out the picture as you did it, I would have thought, oh well, that's as much as they're capable of. But you can do better. I think you should have a go at drawing somebody's portrait from real-life. You will find it much more difficult than simply representing the clichéd characters of the cartoon world. Not that there's anything wrong with cartoons, and you might even find yourself to be gifted in drawing original cartoon characters. But first you must learn to draw from real-life. Will you have a go at this please, and bring me in your results? I don't give out homework in this class, as you know, but I would really like to see how you manage when you sit down and really concentrate on what you can see with your own eyes.'

Morven nodded, somewhat stunned, and scurried away.

BACK HOME, RUTH ASKED MORVEN HOW HER DAY HAD BEEN. 'So-so,' said Morven, 'How was yours?'

'Oh, fine,' said Ruth, 'the greyhounds were back in, for

their flu jabs. Four different cats, every one of them with fleas – and a tortoise. And a budgie.'

'Mrs Morrison says I've to draw a portrait,' said Morven.

'A portrait?'

'Yeah.'

'You could show her all the portraits you made for the beanstalk,' suggested Ruth.

'Well yes,' said Morven, 'but I think she would find them a bit … childish. They don't really count as portraits. I think.' She paused; she'd been so proud of her beanstalk! Maybe she wasn't such a brilliant artist after all? 'She wants me to draw somebody from real-life, like with me just sitting in front of them looking at the face and drawing what I can see. Exactly what I see.'

'Really?' said Ruth, surprised, 'Like a real artist?' She'd never had to do anything like that at school.

'So, will you sit and let me draw you please? After the dishes,' she added.

Ruth hated having her photo taken never mind having somebody sit in front of her and actually draw her face. She saw herself as plain and dowdy, and really didn't want to have that represented on paper.

'Couldn't you ask Jennifer or Kyle or somebody?'

'Oh no I couldn't! Far too embarrassing,' exclaimed Morven, cringing.

'Well,' said Ruth reluctantly, not wanting to thwart Morton's enthusiasm, 'so long as you promise to make me look nice.'

'But that's the whole point! I've got to draw you exactly as I see you,' said Morven.

'Ouch; the things you have to put up with,' thought Ruth.

She gave in and allowed Morven to draw her while she sat watching Pointless on TV later on, the living room in semi shade, and her face in profile rather than straight on. Morven scribbled away, and found it very difficult, but eventually managed to produce something which she thought would have to do. 'I'll just try another one,' she said, moving herself over to Ruth's other side and starting again. 'I don't suppose it'll matter if I take two pictures into Mrs Morrison instead of just the one.' But she was feeling a bit frustrated with what she was producing – it didn't seem to her to be very artistic. Still, she knew she needed to learn, and she liked Mrs Morrison and wanted to please her. She worked painstakingly, in complete silence, until she got to the point where she didn't know how to make it any better, and threw her pencil down. She sat up on the sofa beside Ruth to watch the rest of Pointless and then remembered something. 'By the way,' she asked, 'have we got the car back yet?'

'No,' sighed Ruth, 'I don't know if we'll be getting it back at all. I have to speak to the mechanic tomorrow night, and he'll tell me how much it would cost to fix it. But it's such an ancient old banger, and I think it may have seen its last.'

'Oh no ... So, will we have to buy a new car?'

'What with?'

They fell into silence – Ruth despairing about being stuck in Flegg without her own four wheels; and Morven wondering, as she gazed at the telly, whether she was going to have to fall back on her mother's teaching and reacquaint herself with shoplifting. Not that you could steal anything very valuable from the shops, working on your own - and it would have to be Kinbuckie on school lunchtimes, because she would be caught in no time in Flegg. But maybe if she could acquire a few things and sell them in the playground, or at the back of the school bus, she would be able to slip the odd fiver into Aunt Ruth's purse. How many fivers does it take to buy a new car, she wondered? Then she had another idea.

As the credits rolled at the end of the programme, Morven slipped her jacket on and said to Ruth, 'I need to nip along to Jennifer's to get some info about homework for tomorrow. I forgot to write down the page number. For maths.'

'Well be quick then,' said Ruth, 'it'll be dark in half an hour.' Morven let herself out the front gate and ran as fast as she could down to the labyrinth. Crouching in a hidden corner, she pulled out a page she'd torn from her English jotter, along with her favourite purple felt tip, and scribbled this little note:

Hi Jean-Luc. Morven here. Haven't been in touch for a while because it was school holidays and then new school :(

Have you got any ideas for making money? Our car has broken down. Aunt Ruth hasn't got any money to buy a new one.

Maybe see you around one of these days?

Cheers, Morven

She found the special stone in the labyrinth, where she had buried her own time capsule before the school holidays, and dug it up to bury her note. To her astonishment, she found a pouch, just like the one Aunt Linda had given her – and when she opened it, it contained three silver coins! Jean-Luc must surely have left these for her. He'd guessed what she needed before she'd even asked – how brilliant was that? She examined the coins carefully; they weren't everyday coins so she supposed they must have come from Jean-Luc's era – not that she really knew which era that was. Who would know how to value them? This might be the start of the new car fund – excellent! She quickly scribbled a PS on her note:

Wow, thank you Jean-Luc! That was quick! I owe you one! Bye! Morven

And she buried the note, picking up a few more of those little iron letters which were lying around the hole, added them to the pouch, and ran off home. Ruth called out from the kitchen as Morven was hanging up her jacket, 'Is that you back Morven?'

'Uh huh! I got what I needed from Jennifer. I'm away upstairs now. See you later.'

'Okay. Bring your homework down when it's finished, for me to check.'

Left in peace, Ruth decided to phone Linda and invite her down sometime soon. Linda had agreed – somewhat cautiously, Ruth thought – to come and visit them at Flegg. But, right now, she was busy helping to organise an art exhibition, and they hadn't set the date yet. With a sinking feeling, Ruth realised she probably wouldn't be able to collect Linda off the train in Kinbuckie – Linda would have to get the bus from there to Flegg. It made it quite a long journey, because the buses and trains didn't coincide very well. However, that's just the way it was going to be from now on, so Ruth told herself she might as well get used to it. No point moaning.

Nevertheless, she wanted to get to know Aunt Linda better. She felt that the older woman, in her quiet way, would be a safe person to confide in. Obviously, she hadn't been able to explain all of Morven's story to Aunt Linda when they were visiting her in Arbroath – not with Morven earwigging every word. But Ruth felt it would be helpful to share the story, and the ongoing impact on young Morven's behaviour. And maybe Linda could help her understand what had gone so badly wrong with Alison and Aileen, that ended up in such terrible experiences for Morven and her little brother Fergus, who had died as a result of Aileen's neglect.

Part of her felt it would be better just to forget all those horrible things from the past, but she knew that it was unrealistic to think that Morven could have recovered so easily. She knew there would be many more storms to come. She picked up her phone.

CHAPTER FIVE

Arthur, the Flegg blacksmith, was delighted to see Jean-Luc. 'Old friend! Come in! Look who's here Kate!' he shouted into the interior of their cottage. His wife and mother-in-law took no notice, being heavily engaged in the gossip from Earnside. Various rumours had flown across the hillside and down the valley in the last year, and they had a new source in the factor's housekeeper. Arthur hated the rumours but he was keen for an update - and who better than the young French lad to give him a reliable account? He brought two flagons of ale, and he and Jean-Luc crossed the yard to the forge where they sat by the dying embers, safely private from any intrusion.

'Well, John laddie,' said the blacksmith, 'I'm right pleased to see thee. The stories that keep coming over those hills! I knew they couldn't be true, but there was nobody to tell me any different. When did you get back?'

'Just yesterday, my friend,' said Jean-Luc, delighted to be

given such a warm reception, 'You haven't got any bread or anything here have you?'

'Of course, bread and cheese in the press. It'll take me a minute ...' and Arthur stepped across the courtyard for provisions. When he returned, his face was creased in concentration, 'What's going on up the hill, then?'

'It's a long story,' said Jean-Luc, 'I don't know where to begin.'

'Well, you can start with telling me what happened last year to your steward, up at Glenmiglo,' said the blacksmith, 'There were all sorts of tales at the time, and all involving you – I couldn't believe them – but it seems to be all hushed up.'

Jean-Luc drew a breath, 'I was chasing him, because he had beaten up his daughter, and a sea eagle swooped down, and he fell over the edge of the quarry,' said Jean-Luc, 'I didn't realise the quarry was so close.'

'Never! Those sea eagles are a danger, I've always said so,' said Arthur, 'I will allow, Hugh could be a brute right enough. That quarry! Hugh should have known to keep away from the edge. Horrible way to go, mind. And – did he die straightaway?'

'Yes,' said Jean-Luc, in a small voice, 'As far as I know.' Not so long ago, he'd have said proudly 'and good riddance to him too!', but he was beginning to understand that - vicious old bastard though Hugh the steward had been - it was no small matter to cause a man to die.

'But you didn't kill him?' queried Arthur.

Jean-Luc shook his head.

'That's what people are saying, you know. I told them it

couldn't be true. You know what people are like when they get a story in their heads. I stuck up for you – but I have to admit, I knew you were handy with your fists, and I suppose if you got riled it wasn't an impossibility.'

'I didn't exactly kill him,' said Jean-Luc, 'but to be honest I might have done if I'd got to him before the sea eagle did. I suppose that's a bad thing. I've never been very good at seeing beyond the end of my nose,' he muttered in embarrassment. 'Sir Peter sent me away, but I wanted to come back to see Mairi.'

'Mairi? Hugh's eldest? Well I never!' The blacksmith had been thinking that Jean-Luc, if he really wasn't a killer, could make a great husband for his niece. Was this now a lost cause?

'Yes, Mairi,' said Jean-Luc, 'and now I have learned that she has had a baby...'

'Yes, I heard that too – who is the villain that left her in that state?' bustled Arthur, 'Young girls nowadays, leading a youngster on. And Jess just losing her man, she didn't deserve for her daughter to be used like that.' And then he saw Jean-Luc's face, 'Oh surely not lad, you aren't that stupid are you?'

In the blacksmith's experience, there were only two things a man could do when he got a girl in the family way. If he had the means of supporting her, he should marry her and just get on with it. There were lots of unhappily married men as a result of one night's pleasure, and the blacksmith counted himself as one of them. Twenty years ago, he had felt it was the only honest thing to do – and then of course his father-in-law-to-be had a very persuasive way with him. There wasn't much choice in the end. Never mind, the blacksmith had discharged his responsibilities; and it was more to the pity that the expected child had never materialised, Kate having been taken ill just the week after their wedding. Thereafter, throughout the years, there were no more babies either. Arthur was a practical man. He could thole the unpleasantness at home, with an effort. Even when his mother-in-law moved in. Without children, he was able to reinvest in his business, and work long hours in peace out in the forge.

On the other hand, he didn't have anyone to hand his business onto, and actually he had considered Jean-Luc as a distinct possibility. With Jean-Luc's strength and vigour and goodwill, allied to his niece Sally's kindness and common sense, he could see his business thriving. Were all his hopes for the future coming to nothing?

The other solution that the blacksmith had to offer for someone in Jean-Luc's situation was simply to disappear for a while. It wasn't as if he had any money to support the girl and her babe; she should have known better anyway than lie with him. Sir Peter would surely see her safe enough. Maybe someone else would come forward and claim the baby as their own. It wasn't unknown.

'Get yourself back to France, lad,' the blacksmith offered, 'Wait a while and then return. She'll forget you, and you'll forget her, and then you can marry my niece.'

Jean-Luc stared at him in astonishment. 'Back to France? I've only just come from there!'

'Ah well then, so much the better. Your father will be right pleased with you for the way your skills have developed, I'll wager.'

'Arthur – did you say something about marrying your niece?'

'Never mind that just now, laddie,' said Arthur, 'I spoke out of turn. Tell me about your parents. You were so keen to see them again, they must be very proud of you.'

Jean-Luc nodded yes. Actually, that was the case – his father and mother and brothers had been most impressed at Jean-Luc's new skills. And that was even before he showed them how he could read and write. At that, they were simply disbelieving. 'Is it really that easy?' his brother Thibault had asked, to Jean-Luc's chagrin.

'Easy? It's fiendish hard work,' Jean-Luc had been indignant, 'you've no idea how long it took me to figure it all out. And even now I'm just a beginner.'

Thibault and André had looked at each other. They were going to have to ask their wild younger brother, the family dolt, to teach them how to read and write. How annoying! Jean-Luc chuckled at the memory. He told Arthur about the incident with the *préfet*'s son – the incident which had resulted in him coming to Scotland in the first place. 'I had to make my peace with my father over that,' said Jean-Luc, 'He was still mad at me – he said it could have ruined his business.'

'I daresay it could have,' said Arthur.

'If it hadn't been for my mother's pleading, I reckon my father would have banished me for good. She made him give me a second chance.'

So, after being sent away by Sir Peter, Jean-Luc had returned to France. He had gone back into the forge, and worked with his father and brothers for six months, while secretly figuring out how to return to Flegg, and the Glenmiglo estate, and to his lovely Mairi de la Strath. He had shown his brothers how to read and write, as much as he was able – and it wasn't his fault if André and Thibault had learned a few Scottish words and various errors in the process, but anyhow they got the gist of it. Then one crisp autumn morning, having saved up for the North Sea passage, Jean-Luc had got up before dawn and left without warning, made his way to the Belgian coast, and caught a ship to St Andrews.

'WELL,' THE BLACKSMITH GAVE HIS HONEST OPINION, 'YOU'D BE better there than here right now. Even so, I could do with your help. More horses than ever needing shod. But I can't afford to get on the wrong side of Sir Peter, I need his business too. Why don't you give it another six months, and by that time things will have blown over up the hill, and then you can come back and settle down in Flegg.' He wondered if he should make an outright offer of a job to Jean-Luc; but something held him back. Maybe the lad had a bit more growing up to do. And anyway, Sally was still a bit on the young side. His plans would wait.

Jean-Luc could see that the blacksmith was set on him returning to France, and wasn't going to be budged on his opinion. He also recognised that Mairi needed a safe home and some money coming in - more than he could offer her right now, to his intense regret. Would someone else look after her? He shifted in his seat as he realised it was his fault that her father wouldn't be around to support her. Even if her father's support came at a heavy price. Maybe Arthur was right. Perhaps the best thing he could do right now was to go back home, earn some more money, find a way of convincing Sir Peter to have him back. Then he and Mairi would be able to settle down together with the babe, happy as pigs in shit. 'If I do go away again, will you let me know the news?' he asked Arthur, 'Like whether Sir Peter might ever let me back?'

'How? You know I can't read and write, lad,' said Arthur, 'Don't worry, Sir Peter will come round in due course.'

Jean-Luc said good night to Arthur and strode down the hill to the Abbey ruins, deciding to catch the boat for St Andrews the next day, thence to return to France. He hunkered down in the Slype, away from the wind and managed to catch a few hours' sleep. The next morning, he rose, stretched, ate the remains of the bread and cheese which the blacksmith had given him the night before, and went to the Labyrinth to dig up his purse.

The ferry had arrived at the pier, and he just had time to grab his money and run to catch it – but the purse had disappeared! Perturbed, he lifted a few other stones nearby, thinking perhaps he had mistakenly dug up the wrong stone the night before. However, this was not the case. He was still searching when he heard the hoot of the ferry as it cast away from the pier, bound for St Andrews. He scrabbled again in the original hole and found a little note –

Wow, thank you Jean-Luc! That was quick! I owe you one!
Bye! Morven

Well damnation, if it wasn't that Morven-Martin again! The one who said he needed a strong friend – and now he'd gone off with his entire fortune! What was he going to do now? He would have to find this Morven-Martin, he decided, and figure out once and for all what was going on, and get his three silver coins back, by force if not diplomacy. And he was no diplomat. How to find him?

Jean-Luc spent the rest of the morning gathering plums and selling them around the doorsteps in Flegg. They didn't fetch much – those who were able enough had already been and picked their own plums, plus the ones in the Abbey ruins. However, he earned a shilling to help see him on his way, or at least to get him started on his journey home.

It would be a long walk to St Andrews – Jean-Luc remembered all too well the length of time it had taken him and Joseph to arrive here that very first time, a year or so before. He couldn't afford the ferry now that his coins had been stolen; but it would be an easier and quicker journey if only he had a horse. As he plodded homewards from his last sale of plums, he cut across a field and there, standing at the fence gazing into the Abbey ruins, stood a magnificent black stallion. Jean-Luc gazed in admiration – he'd never seen such a beauty. He pulled a handful of grass and held it out to the beast – he knew an opportunity when he saw one. 'Here, boy,' he enticed the horse, and it turned its big fringed eyes towards him, ready to make friends. Jean-Luc stretched out his hand and scratched its nose. 'You want to help me, boy?' said Jean-Luc, 'Are you ready for an adventure?' And the horse nuzzled his shoulder.

'There are two things I need,' whispered Jean-Luc into the horse's ear, 'First, I need to find a young lad called Martin. Then I need to get to St Andrews. Will you help me?' And the horse simply snorted, in complicity. 'I'll think up a good name for you.' The stallion allowed himself to be led into the Abbey ruins. Jean-Luc patted him down, and gave him some hay. 'You and I are going to wait by the Labyrinth until young Martin appears,' he whispered, 'And then we'll see what's what.'

IN THE CRUSH AND FOG OF THE CENTURIES, THE SCHOOL BUS was invisible to Jean-Luc. However, around mid-afternoon, it trundled in from Kinbuckie, stopped at the bottom of Flegg's main street, and Morven dismounted along with half a dozen other youngsters. She set herself a fast pace towards the Abbey ruins, to check for a response from Jean-Luc before going home. To her surprise, she saw the magnificent stallion Merlin from over-by, standing swatting flies with his big black tail in the Abbey ruins. 'Merlin!' she called, 'How on earth did you get in here?' She and Merlin took a few steps towards each other, when to her intense surprise, she was grabbed from behind and hoisted onto Merlin's broad back. A massive young man with black hair climbed up behind her and muttered in her ear, 'Hello Martin, you and I have to speak.' And, nudging Merlin in his sides, he steered them away up the hill, past the steadings, past a tall line of cherry trees towards the Bear.

Morven kicked and screamed and tried her best to jump off the horse, but she found herself completely penned in by this enormous young man. She had guessed immediately who he was – his rough woollen robe instantly proclaiming him as a visitor from another century. Up until now of course, she had regarded him as a potential friend. So, heart beating like a hammer, she decided she had no other choice than to keep her mouth shut and, as soon as they stopped, try to explain – if she could... it wasn't her strong point.

Otherwise, she would just have to kick him in the balls and run for it.

Jean-Luc pulled up in the shadow of a massive oak tree, and dismounted, hefting his passenger with him. He spun Morven round to take a good look, and his jaw dropped. He spun her around again to make certain. A girl! Whatever next?

CHAPTER SIX

Ruth was looking forward to Morven getting home from school. She had some good news for her — not life-changing good news, but still something which she thought Morven would like, and which she herself was happy about. A neighbour in the next street had asked her whether she would be willing to look after her golden retriever for the weekend. Ruth already knew Duffy because he was a regular visitor at the vets, one of the favourites among her and her colleagues in fact, a gentle, amiable, big softie of a dog. Not the sort of dog that would cause any problems for Suzi and Storm, their two cats. Duffy's owner must have formed a positive opinion of Ruth, and now it seemed she was visiting her grandchildren for the weekend, and couldn't take the dog with her. Ruth was delighted. She was aware that dog-sitting was a service which people were willing to pay for; and perhaps this might be a possibility for her in the future, helping her eke out her finances a bit. On this occasion, she didn't want to be paid, as she was anxious her efforts wouldn't be good enough.

'I'll pay you!' argued the woman.

'Not at all!' insisted Ruth. So, they had agreed that Duffy would be delivered on Friday night at six o'clock, and would stay with them until Sunday night at the same time. Ruth was honoured to be trusted for this and was pretty sure Morven would also be delighted. But what was keeping Morven? She knew the school bus had passed through, because she had seen some other kids straggling along the street five minutes earlier. She took a walk down the garden path to the gate, looking to left and right - no sign. Up on Bear Hill there seemed to be a bit of activity — probably just maintenance work. No sign of Morven though. Returning to the kitchen, she drained the macaroni through a colander, poured it back into the pot, and stirred in a jar of tomato sauce. Was it too late to phone the school and make sure Morven had got on the school bus? She transferred the pasta to a Pyrex dish and grated some cheese over before putting it in the oven. Morven ought to be home in time to set the table. Where had she got to this time?

Morven was still up the hill with Jean-Luc: information which would have reassured Ruth not one bit. Merlin the horse stood there, pawing at the ground, breathing hard after the strenuous climb uphill with his double burden. Morven squared up to Jean-Luc, heart hammering but chin raised, hands clenched and fists up, ready to defend herself if need be.

'A girl!' uttered Jean-Luc, aghast. That Morven might be a

girl had never ever occurred to him, and he felt completely confused and horrified that he had seized a young girl and dragged her away by horseback. Anyone who had witnessed them would have taken him for an utter villain. Had she tricked him? Was she pretending to be a boy?

'And? Your point is?' hissed Morven, 'Why did you grab me like that? I could have you done for child abduction.' The panic of her experience with Jade and the creep Mark, in Glencadam car park, was ever raw. Even if creep Mark and Jean-Luc were entirely different propositions, it was still awful to feel so helpless. 'What are you doing here anyway?' she demanded, 'All the times I needed you, and you were nowhere to be found! What has suddenly changed?'

Jean-Luc was not one to back off in a conflict, but he would never engage in a battle with a girl. Or rather, not knowingly. The way Morven was dressed seemed designed to deliberately confuse him. Where was the long skirt, the apron? Certainly, she had long hair, but it was tied back in a way which could make her easily pass for a boy. Morven broke into his thoughts, 'Which century are you from anyway?' she demanded.

'Century?' he repeated foolishly.

Morven stared at him. It seemed he didn't know very much. Maybe he'd never been to school. Frustrated, she tried to explain, 'Like, we're in the 21st century now... or at least I was when I got off the bus earlier on.'

'The bus?' said Jean-Luc, 'What's a bus?'

How to explain? Morven realised they had a lot of talking to do to try and understand each other.

'Are you sure you're not going to try and abduct me again?'

'I wasn't trying to abduct you!'

'Yes you were! Look,' Morven suggested, 'if we walk slowly back down the hill to Flegg, so that I'm not too late home for Aunt Ruth, and if you promise to keep your distance from me, we can try and explain things to each other.'

'All right,' agreed Jean-Luc. Then he remembered something, 'But you stole my purse!'

'Purse? I did not!'

'With three silver coins. I left them for safekeeping, and you took them.'

'Ah yes,' said Morven, realising what he was on about, 'yes that's right, I did. I thought they were a gift.'

'Well, they're all the money I have in the world,' said Jean-Luc, 'and I really need them back.'

'I'm skint too,' said Morven, 'I need that money.'

They started walking down the hill, six feet apart, discussing the purpose of silver coins and their ownership, not noticing when Merlin peeled away towards his own paddock. The Steeple bells were chiming for six o'clock when they arrived back down at the Abbey, and Morven knew she would be in trouble. However, they had exchanged some important information, and had begun to understand where each other stood in their shared adventure. She knew she would have to get his coins back. Though how, she hadn't a clue.

'Did you steal Merlin?'

'I didn't know his name was Merlin. No, I didn't really steal him, I just borrowed him. He came to me, in fact. He just appeared when I was in dire need of transport. I'll return him as soon as I've finished with him.'

'Have you stolen other things?' asked Morven.

'Not really. I don't think so. Only if I needed them more than the other person did.'

'I'm going to have to steal some things to make some money for Auntie Ruth,' said Morven, 'her car's in the garage and probably will never run again. She hasn't got enough money to have it fixed, or to buy another one.'

'Well,' said Jean-Luc, 'my advice is that if you're stealing something, don't get caught, and make it worth your while. Like a horse – that was fun, and we did no harm. You enjoyed it too, didn't you?' He turned, expecting to address Merlin. 'Gone! As quietly as he arrived!'

Morven stored Jean-Luc's advice in her mind as a way of figuring out future moral dilemmas. Have fun, do no harm, don't get caught. 'So, what are you up to now? Will you be sticking around?'

Jean-Luc's face fell a little. 'I have to go back to France,' he said, 'and then I hope that Sir Peter will take me back, and I will get to be with my Mairi de la Strath.'

'Sir Peter? Mairi?' said Morven, 'Who are they?'

'Well you must know Sir Peter, he's the landowner. And Mairi… She's a lovely woman, a girl really, and I want to spend the rest of my life with her. She even has my baby. But I kind of brought trouble to her and her family, so I'm not welcome at the moment. Sir Peter needs to forget my part in her father's death, and then I hope he'll have me back.'

Morven said nothing; this was serious trouble right enough. A part in someone's death? Jean-Luc continued, 'If Sir Peter won't have me back, I'm hoping maybe my friend Arthur, the blacksmith, will take me in. Do you know him?'

'Arthur the blacksmith,' repeated Morven, 'no, of course I

don't know him, Dumbo, there's about 500 years between him and me!'

Jean-Luc sighed, 'You're cleverer than I am. Are you going to give me my coins back?'

'I'm sorry,' said Morven, 'I truly am. I sold them.'

'Sold them!'

'I'll give you the money I got for them,' Morven said reluctantly, rummaging in her pocket and producing a five-pound note and a pound coin. She handed them to Jean-Luc, who took them and examined them carefully. 'These are no use to me,' he said, 'the boatman won't accept them for my crossing to France.' They looked at each other sheepishly.

'I'm so sorry,' said Morven, 'I just thought you'd left them for me. If you come back here one day, I'll make it up to you, I promise. I owe you. What are you going to do now?'

'I'll just have to earn some more money somehow,' sighed Jean-Luc. 'If I can get hold of Merlin again, I'll get him to take me to St Andrews. Otherwise it'll be a long walk, but that would be cheaper than waiting for the boat down the river.' Morven held out her hand. 'Travel safely, Jean-Luc, and let me know when you get back. In the usual way of course.' They nodded. 'One final thing,' she said, 'your girl-friend Mairi – what does she look like?'

'Oh, she's beautiful,' said Jean-Luc, 'far too beautiful for an oaf like me. But I think she loves me just the same. She has long auburn hair, and the most beautiful sparkling green eyes.'

'I've seen her,' said Mairi, 'here,' and she showed him some letters from the printing press which she carried in her pocket. Of course, he recognised them instantly. 'Look what happens when I hold them tight in my hand,' she said, and she rubbed them gently between her palms until they warmed and vibrated, and suddenly there was a vision of Mairi standing in front of Morven, two little pink creatures in her arms, a smile on her face and tears in her eyes. 'See?'

But Jean-Luc didn't know what she was on about – he could see nothing.

'She's got two little piglets I think,' said Morven. 'Is she a farmer or something?'

'Sort of. She works at the big house at Glenmiglo.'

'Well, she looks happy and sad at the same time,' said Morven. 'If I were you, I wouldn't go back to France, I'd get right back up that hill and visit Mairi. I think she needs you.' Jean-Luc's heart was sore. 'How I wish I could,' he said, 'but I have nothing to offer.'

'Oh well,' said Morven, as the vision of Mairi faded into thin air, 'that's a pity.' She lifted her fist and held it up to Jean-Luc who looked completely puzzled. 'This,' she said, and showed him how to fist-bump. 'Good luck on your journey. See you when you get back, I hope.' And she turned and headed for home.

Ruth was at her wits end.

CHAPTER SEVEN

Jess was in the dairy, cranking the handle to churn the butter. But it wasn't coming easily, as she realised when she lifted the lid off for a peek. Sometimes, with butter, the weather defeated you; she bent her back to the job and just kept going — nothing else for it. Sir Peter and Lady Janet must have their butter. Just at that, Lady Janet walked into the dairy and into Jess's line of sight, holding her little boy John in her arms. John's cheek was scarlet, and he was grizzling into his mother's shoulder. 'Teething,' Lady Janet said to Jess.

'Oh, what a shame,' said Jess, 'have you tried catnip?'

'Catnip! Does it work?' asked Lady Janet, 'I've tried chamomile without much success, but I've never heard of catnip for a child.'

'I'd give it a try. There's a patch behind the hayshed – I'll just go and get it,' but Lady Janet held her back.

'Wait, I'll get it in a minute, but first...'

'... you steep the fresh leaves in boiled water for 20

minutes then strain it and cool it and give him a spoonful at a time. It worked well for my Davey. What's the matter?'

Lady Janet paused. 'I was wondering how you're getting on without your girls?'

'Ah well. You know how it is. Nothing else for it. Beth and Peggy were both excited to be away, and I've no doubt they'll work hard enough.'

'That's good then. And... what about Mairi? Is she coping with her twins?'

Jess's face fell. 'I don't know what to make of the girl,' she confessed. 'She has this blind faith that that French boy will come back and take up his duties where he left off. She hardly knows him! But you'd think he was the boy next door, the way she trusts him. I reckon we'll never see him again.'

Lady Janet sighed, 'Yes, I'm sorry Sir Peter was so quick to send him away. Of course, he didn't know that Mairi was bearing his child. You must know that he had a great deal of respect for your Hugh and felt it was only decent to send the youngster away for a while. Even if he didn't exactly push your husband over the edge of the quarry, probably Hugh wouldn't have been anywhere near it if Jean-Luc hadn't chased him.'

'That's what I think too,' said Jess. 'Hugh knew his way around these hills like the back of his hand. Mind you, it's true that he had given our Mairi a good hiding that night, for no reason that I can fathom. You can understand the young lad being angry with him. It's all a sorry mess.'

'What's she going to do? Is she keeping the babies?'

'That's her intention. Although,' added Jess grimly, 'she might come to a different conclusion when her milk runs out, and she has no way of feeding them. It's not as if I have anything to fall back on. I can't afford to keep them in food and clothing.' The two women were silent for a while and Jess resumed her churning of the butter.

'Maybe she could help us here, up at the big house, and bring the babies with her?' said Lady Janet. 'Maybe as a nursemaid? I have my hands full with Little John here, and the others still need a lot of attention.'

'You've been so kind to her already,' said Jess. 'If only she could see how lucky she's been.'

'There's another thing too,' said Lady Janet. 'Young Douglas from the next estate has been asking after her.'

'The young Douglas?' This was a surprise for Jess. She'd been too wretched to notice it on the day of Hugh's fall into the quarry, but Lady Janet had mentioned before that the young Douglas, who had followed Mairi down into the quarry to bring up her father's body, had commented on her daughter's agility and cool head. 'But that would never work,' she shrugged.

'I know. Too big a difference in the backgrounds,' said Lady Janet, 'And I believe the young Douglas is betrothed to a cousin of his on the Dundee side.' She paused. 'It's not a love match,' she added.

Jess looked up sharply. 'And what does he want with our Mairi?'

Lady Janet pursed her lips. 'Forgive me if I'm speaking out of turn,' she said, 'I just thought it might not do young Mairi's future chances any harm if she were to be nice to him the next time he visits.'

Jess went back to the churning, saying nothing. 'Oh well, I'd better find that catnip then,' said Lady Janet. And she went off with the grizzling John. Jess's jaw was set. What was to become of them?

MAIRI WAS SUPERVISING THE YOUNGER SERVANTS IN CARRYING out the cleaning of the Great Hall. There was another feast coming up, and the servants hadn't fully dusted the hall down all summer. The plan was to do all the cleaning this week so that next week they could organise the stabling outside, and in the kitchens, they could get started on the cooking. Mairi had laid her twins — little Archie and little Fiona — on a rug in the far corner, gurgling quietly at each other. On the whole they were contented babes, and Mairi had learned that she was very lucky in this respect; Lady Janet herself had told her about all the birthings that ended in either mother or baby dead, or catching all kinds of illnesses and often not surviving beyond infancy. Mairi's blood run cold at such a prospect.

She was training the young servants to take a turn with Archie and Fiona, hoping to free herself up for some more vigorous work. Sitting nursing babies wasn't really her strong point — it was too slow. However, nobody else could see to the feeding of them, and she looked forward to the day when she could hand them over to be fed gruel from a spoon.

Sir Peter strode into the hall, looked around, nodded and went out again. Mairi wondered whether he ever realised just how much work was involved in these huge gatherings, which he insisted on holding every few months. Not that it was any business of hers, and she knew that most of the visitors brought along various gifts for the kitchen or the farm when they arrived. She was beginning to appreciate the value of money — something she had barely noticed in the past — and how the estate staff kept the wheels turning, bringing warmth, comfort and roasted hog to Sir Hugh and Lady Janet, and gruel to the workers. Nobody complained. She had been born into poverty, and wouldn't have expected anything else. However, now that she had two little babies to think of, she was beginning to appreciate her mother's terror that if they didn't have enough money, the unthinkable might have to be thought about. For the moment, she wouldn't even name it in her heart.

A WEEK LATER, MAIRI WAS BACK IN THE GREAT HALL supervising her small troop of servants in lugging the heavy oak tables into place. Then there was firewood to be stacked up in baskets by the two great fireplaces at either end of the hall, fresh candles to be set in place, silver to be polished, dishes to be cleaned and set out, and then fresh herbs to be strewn underfoot. In the kitchen, her mother had already made a stack of pies, and arranged for the hog to be hoisted on to its spit. There were another two days' worth of steady labour involved in getting the feast ready. 'What's the celebration anyway?' Mairi asked her mother that night.

'Something to do with Queen Mary,' said Jess, 'She is back on the throne, and this is to wish her success — and to pray for calmer times for the monks. Anyway,' she said, changing the subject, 'you'd better have a bath tomorrow night to be nice and clean for the big day.'

'A bath? Me?' Mairi stared at her mother in disbelief. 'The burn is freezing cold at this time of year.'

'Well, you know what I mean. Get down to the burn with

a bucket of water and have a good old scrub, including your hair – it's all tangled and greasy, you'd think you'd been dragged through a hedge backwards. You've got to look your best as well you know.'

'Whatever for? I'm not going to be on show, am I?'

'Well, you just don't know who's looking, do you?' snapped Jess. 'All those gentlemen. One of them may take a shine to you.'

'What on earth are you saying, mother?' uttered Mairi. 'You know perfectly well that they'll all be wedded or betrothed to rich ladies. They're not going to be interested in the likes of me. Unless they're bringing their servants with them?'

'Well, I'm just saying, you never know, that's all,' said Jess, wishing she'd kept her mouth shut. 'In our position, you can't afford to be choosy.'

'No, but they can!' Mairi didn't know what had got into her mother. As if anyone cared what she looked like! On the morning of the event, she got up early to feed the babies, and was pulling on her shift when her mother threw her a bar of soap and told her to get washed. 'I'll see to the babes just now,' said Jess, 'and get them dressed. You go and make yourself look presentable. And that's an order!' She added, more softly, 'Lady Janet particularly requested it.'

Defeated, but still puzzled, Mairi did as she was bid, then headed downhill with the babies to get organised for the guests arriving at lunchtime. She didn't see why she should be the only one clean and tidy, so she bullied all the young servants into having an extra wash as well, and the result was that by the time the guests were arriving, the house staff were unusually pink and primped, lined up along the driveway to greet the Lords and Ladies.

It was quite a spectacle. Such an array of horses! Some beautiful fine thoroughbred beasts, some lovely geldings, a couple of drays, and a few little Shetland ponies, perfect little beasts for fetching children and luggage. Mairi arranged the staff to collect cloaks and was herself hanging up a fine fur stole in the back porch when she felt a hand on her waist from behind. She whirled round and came face-to-face with one of the guests. What a nerve! 'I think you'll find the Great Hall is through that other door,' she smiled icily, pointing. The gentleman bowed, 'I am much obliged, young lady,' he said, 'however I wished to enquire as to your comfort in the wake of that sad disaster last Spring.'

She looked at him, puzzled. 'Don't you recognise me?' he prompted. And then recognition dawned.

'Are you the gentleman who helped me bring my father's body up from the quarry?' she enquired.

The young Douglas gazed at this beautiful young woman, displaying such composure. He had seen her on a day when surely, she had been under enormous stress, and yet she had never put a foot wrong in the scrambling out of that treacherous canyon, carrying such a trying load. She may have been a servant; dressed in a rough though spotless apron; but in his eyes, she was fit,strong, clever and elegant. 'I am your neighbour, Richmond Douglas. At your service,' and he bowed again.

Mairi curtsied, not knowing how to deal with this situation. Nobody had ever bowed at her in all her life. She knew that the gulf socially between herself and the guest was unbridgeable. What might he be after? Six months ago, when she was more naïve, she would have been even more at a loss. Now, having had to endure some close questioning and lewd remarks from people curious about the parenthood of her babies, she had a fair idea what this gentleman might want. But she was saving herself for Jean-Luc. She said nothing, but kept her wary eyes locked on the young man.

'I have taken the liberty,' he continued, 'of fetching you a small gift.'

A gift? From a member of the landed classes, to a servant girl? Unheard of. This could only spell trouble.

'It's just out here at the back door,' he added. 'Would you like to come and see it?'

Mairi didn't know how to say no to someone of the young Douglas's standing. It went against everything her parents had ever taught her about knowing her place. She dropped another curtsy and followed the young Douglas as he led the way to the back door behind the kitchen, wary that he might seize her in some kind of embrace. How did he know where the kitchen was anyway? A wooden crate had been stashed out the back, and the Douglas gestured towards this, inviting her to open it. As she prised off the lid of the crate, there was a squeaking and snuffling from inside. To her astonishment, two little pink piglets squealed and wriggled. She laughed out loud. 'Piglets!' she exclaimed, 'How magnificent!' and then remembered herself. 'I'm so sorry,' she said, 'They are beautiful. But I cannot possibly accept them.'

'Don't you have anywhere to keep them?' he asked.

'Oh yes,' said Mairi, 'we have a little paddock behind the cottage...'

'And would your mother not find them useful?'

Mairi pictured her mother's face when she turned up at

home tonight with two little piglets. Nothing could, she was sure, please her mother more. Hams and bacon and black pudding for next winter! Trotters for jelly! Bristles even, for brushes! The image in her mind of an approving smile on her mother's face was very compelling. She wondered whether it would in fact be acceptable to keep this gift. What would people think? She sneaked another look at the little piglets, snuffling in their bed of straw, and realised that she didn't want to give them back. 'Sir,' she murmured, 'my mother would be more than delighted. As would I,' she added faintly.

'Well then, that's settled,' said the young Douglas, 'I have cleared it with Sir Peter and Lady Janet. They are of the opinion that a pair of piglets will be most valuable to your family in the unfortunate circumstances in which you find yourself. And so, I commend them to you.'

Mairi bit her lip. What would he expect from her in return? Had her mother tricked her, making such a fuss about getting washed this morning? She was gazing at the young Douglas as these thoughts went through her head, and he caught her eye and smiled, catching her off guard, and said, 'please. Just take them. One of our sows produced a big healthy litter; it's a small gift from our farm, and I hope they will bring you joy.'

His voice sounded kind. Mairi remembered that when her milk ran out, not so long in the future, she would struggle to feed her own babies. Reluctantly, she dropped a curtsy, bracing herself for his move, 'Thank you kindly, Sir,' she said, 'I will tell my mother and she will be most grateful.'

He gazed at her, one eyebrow raised, bowed again, and strode off back through the kitchen area to the Great Hall and the celebrations. Mairi exhaled and bent to admire the piglets. Her piglets. She was a piglet-owner! Her mother's machinations hadn't been so disastrous.

It would be fun to show them to Jean-Luc she thought, if they were still small when he returned, and if they hadn't yet been eaten.

CHAPTER EIGHT

Dusk was falling as Jean-Luc whistled across the field and Merlin came trotting towards him. He patted the horse on the shoulder and scratched him between the ears, and gave him a turnip he'd picked up from the abbey kailyard. Merlin lifted his lips and snickered. 'We're going to St Andrews, you and me,' said Jean-Luc. 'You'll have to find your own way home, but I'm sure you'll manage that, won't you, you clever beast?' Merlin turned big trusting eyes on the young man, who clambered onto his broad back. Horse and man were made for each other. They set off at a steady canter, heading eastwards.

Back in 21st century Flegg, Morven had been grounded. She couldn't figure out a believable story to offer Ruth, so she had simply told her she had dropped in at Kyle's. When Ruth phoned Kyle's Dad and found out that this was not the case, she was furious. And so, this was it – for the first time since Morven had come back to live with her, Ruth had resorted to grounding as the only way she could think of to make Morven behave more responsibly. Even though she didn't really believe in punishment. It made her feel like a careless parent. But it wasn't just about being late back, it was about telling lies – to her, of all people! When she was only trying to protect her niece. What else could she do?

'And anyway,' she nagged, 'who were you with? You know there are creeps out there, surely I don't have to remind you of that!'

Morven said nothing. In her pocket, her fingers fiddled with the little metal letters, and she could feel them warming up and vibrating. It was a great comfort to her to feel connected with generations long in the past; sometimes they seemed more straightforward than those in the immediate present.

'Just go up to your room then,' said Ruth. 'You can come down at nine o'clock for supper, and then straight to bed. For the next week, I want you straight in after school, and homework done, and there will be no going out in the evenings. I have to be able to trust you.'

As Morven stomped off upstairs, Ruth reflected that this parenting lark was much harder than anybody could imagine. She hated the idea that Morven might get into trouble again, or put herself at further risk. And even more so, that she appeared to be powerless to prevent it. At supper time, she served up the rather dried out macaroni bake which, in her anxiety, she had forgotten about earlier on. 'By the way,' she said to Morven, 'we're having a dog for the weekend.'

'Oh yeah?' replied Morven cautiously. 'Which dog? Rosa?'

'Duffy. You don't know her yet. She's a golden retriever.'

'A pup?'

'Eight-year-old.'

'Are we allowed to keep her all weekend?' asked Morven. She had often begged Ruth to let one of the surgery dogs stay overnight.

'It's a private arrangement. Nothing to do with work.'

'Oh. Okay then.' Morven finished her supper and went upstairs to bed.

THE WEEKEND PASSED MORE PLEASANTLY THAN EITHER RUTH or Morven had dared hope. They had come to an awkward agreement that there would be no more discussion about the late arrival home the other night. Ruth secretly wondered whether she had overreacted; and Morven understood only too well why her great-aunt was anxious. She didn't want to tell her any lies, and knew that she couldn't possibly explain about Jean-Luc, the phantom Frenchman whom her aunt feared so much. So, she retreated into the only solution she could think of – silence.

Having Duffy with them eased the atmosphere considerably, and Morven took her full share of walking the retriever in the park and around the Abbey ruins, launching ball after ball from a catcher for miles as the big yellow dog bounced happily around, fetching the balls and bringing them right back, her enormous tail swishing to and fro behind her. No sign of Jean-Luc; Morven had no idea when she might see him again. On the Sunday night, when Duffy's owner came to collect her, she handed Ruth a bottle of wine. Ruth was delighted, 'Oh, you shouldn't have,' she said, 'I told you I didn't want to be paid!'

'Well, it's just a little minding,' said the woman, 'I'm

grateful to you. Will you mind if I ask you again another time? Only, I want to pay you next time.'

'We'd love to, wouldn't we Morven,' said Ruth. Morven nodded. She knew how much a bottle of wine cost at the Co-op, and she knew how much it would cost to keep a dog in kennels for the weekend, because she had looked it up on the Internet. She secretly thought her aunt was far too generous – but then, that was her Auntie Ruth's way, and if it wasn't for her generosity, Morven would probably be living in some horrific care home somewhere – so she said nothing.

That night, after Morven had gone to bed, Ruth checked her purse to see if she had enough to buy rolls at the baker's in the morning. She knew exactly how much money she had, but it was always worth having another look. To her surprise, she found an extra six pounds in her purse. That was strange. She poured herself a glass of wine and wondered where the money might have come from and decided she must have miscounted the last time she had checked. In any case, it was good that the weekend had gone so well. Maybe Morven was settling down again. Maybe they could save the family fortunes by dog walking.

A shiny blue Nissan Micra pulled up outside Ruth's front gate, right in the spot where Ruth's ancient and trusty model would be sitting if it weren't still in the garage, awaiting a verdict. Out stepped a young woman dressed in faded black, with long, blonde hair tied back in a severe ponytail. Ruth peeked from behind the curtain. She was ready for Astrid; everything clean and polished. Mugs out on a tray. Morven warned to be on her best behaviour. 'I'll be upstairs if you need me,' said Morven, disappearing sharpish and closing her door firmly. Ruth listened at the foot of the stair and as expected, heard Morven's door being reopened a crack – she'd be listening throughout to the conversation. To Morven, Astrid represented all kinds of awkward memories and unpleasant possibilities.

Recently, Astrid's visits had reverted to her monthly minimum statutory requirement. She took her duties seriously. Too seriously for Ruth's comfort – but, as she had to keep reminding herself, she just had to put up with it. It was one of those things that went along with looking after other people's children. Especially if there was a Children's Hearing requirement in place.

'Tea, Astrid?' she offered. 'I have chamomile.'

'Chamomile, yes, thank you Ruth,' said Astrid. 'So, how are things with Morven?'

Bloody hell, straight in for the kill.

'Do you need a cushion?' Ruth stalled. Would she or wouldn't she tell Astrid about Morven being late home the other night? Such a fuss would be made, and really, in retrospect, she wasn't sure whether she might have overreacted. The real difficulty, in Ruth's eyes, was that she hadn't managed to find out where Morven had been. She didn't want to share this with the social worker – what good could come of it? It showed her up as a totally inadequate parent-substitute. So, she fudged a little, mentally crossing her fingers while Astrid gazed at her, waiting for a reply. 'Fine,' she said, 'she's getting on fine.'

'Any problems at school?' asked Astrid.

'Generally okay,' said Ruth. 'She's a bit sketchy with her

homework, but it gets done after a fashion. She still lacks confidence. Her art teacher is taking an interest in her.'

'That's good,' said Astrid, 'Morven must be happy about that. How's the family tree going?'

Ruth told Astrid about the visit to Arbroath, and meeting up with Morven's Great Aunt Linda, and how well it had gone.

'That's good,' said Astrid again, taking notes in a little notebook. 'Will you be seeing Linda again?'

'She's coming down for a visit, not this weekend but next,' said Ruth.

'I wonder if I should have her police-checked at this point?' said Astrid, thinking out loud. 'I'd better check with my team manager.'

'Police-checked?' Ruth was shocked at the prospect. 'She's my aunt! It's not as if she's a stranger.'

'Well, she has been up till now, hasn't she?' said Astrid sweetly. 'To Morven, at any rate. Anyway, she may become an important person in Morven's life, with a lot of access to her, and you know that you can never be too careful these days. I'll look into it. Don't worry, it won't be intrusive. Just a question of filling in a form or two.' She saw Ruth's face and added, 'I'll do the filling in, you won't have to.'

'I'm perfectly capable of filling in forms, thank you,' said Ruth, stung. 'I'm just a bit... shocked that you think a close relative has to be checked out. I mean, surely family life is the very thing that Morven needs?'

'Yes, well, I don't make up the rules,' said Astrid crisply. 'What else have you been up to?'

Ruth let it go for the moment. 'Well,' she said, 'we had a dog staying over the weekend. A golden retriever. As you know, Morven loves animals, so it went very well. I'm thinking of starting a dog walking business.' In retrospect, she wondered why she had even mentioned this – she should have known that Astrid would want to know all the ins and outs.

'A dog walking business? Would Morven be taking part in that?'

'Probably. She loves walking the dogs.'

'Mustn't have child labour. And are you sure you're not taking on too much?'

'Well, it's just an idea at this stage...'

'Children in Morven's position can be so insecure, and you wouldn't believe how easy it is for them to get upset and start acting out all over again,' said Astrid.

Ruth said nothing, but her pursed lips said it all. Astrid didn't notice as she was writing down some detail or other in her notebook. 'Are you thinking of giving up your job at the vet's?' asked Astrid.

'Of course not! I really need the money. That's why I'm thinking about doing the dog walking – Morven and I are often walking dogs anyway, at night time.'

'Well, my advice would be to wait awhile and give Morven a bit longer to settle down. You don't want to undo all the excellent work that you've done up till now, do you? Anyway, as you know, I have to complete an assessment for you as a kinship carer. There will be a little extra financial support then, so you won't have to think about taking on so much.'

Ruth gritted her teeth. 'Shall I give Morven a call,' she suggested, and went to the foot of the stairs. 'Morven! Come down and have a word with Astrid!'

Morven came thundering down the stairs and threw herself into an armchair opposite the sofa where Astrid sat, smiling indulgently. Give the woman her due, thought Ruth, Astrid did try very hard to get Morven to engage in conversation – but Morven was sticking to her usual monosyllabic policy when dealing with officials, and after an uncomfortable five minutes or so, Astrid got up to leave. 'Thank goodness she's gone,' said Morven, as she watched the little blue Micra putt away up the street.

'Don't be so damned rude! She's got to write reports about you, you know, for the children's hearing and all that. What she says, goes.'

'I wasn't rude!'

'Yes, you were!'

'How? What did I say that was rude?'

'It's not what you said, it was the way you refused to even try to make conversation.'

'Conversation!' said Morven, unimpressed. 'Am I still grounded?'

Ruth gave in. 'Be back in half an hour; and not a minute later.' She leaned against the kitchen counter, and asked herself – how come a woman half her age owned a shiny new car, and had the right to come in here and order her around in her own home? And her own car's fate still in the balance? It was a bitter pill to swallow. Where had she gone wrong in her own life, that she had to put up with the likes of Astrid?

Beth and Peggy were fizzling with excitement, desperate to see each other, as they hurried from different directions towards their meeting point – the lightning-blasted oak at the end of Nine Bells Road. Never in all their lives had they been parted before; they were like peas in a pod, knowing what the other would say before the words were spoken. When they had dreamt of the future, it was always a future they would spend together. Somehow, neither of them had foreseen how difficult this parting would be for them – harder, indeed, than leaving home. When they caught sight of each other in the distance, they ran even faster, nearly knocking each other over with delight when they met. So much to tell!

When the initial excitement was over, they ran an eye over each other's appearance. 'New dress!' said Beth, twirling. 'Do you like it? It used to be the factor's daughter's. All I had to do was take the hem up a bit. It fits perfectly!'

'Oh yes, it's smart,' said Peggy. 'Good colour for us, is she a redhead too? Imagine you wearing the factor's daughter's dress! What's it like working with him? Aren't you scared?'

'I hardly ever see him,' said Beth. 'His wife is all right, kind of stern though. I have to call her Mrs Cunningham, or just Ma'am. I think she likes me well enough. Most of the time, though, I'm just working with Agnes, the housekeeper. She's very strict. How about you?'

'Yes, it's good,' said Peggy. 'Quite a lot of work in the dairy, just as well we've watched Mother and Mairi there plenty times. Here, let me show you this,' and she unwrapped her shawl and showed her sister her blouse. 'It belonged to one of the other maids,' she said, 'who left it behind when she had to leave last year. Nice to get some new things, isn't it? What kind of work are you doing?'

'Oh, a lot of sweeping out ashes and carrying firewood and stuff like that. Scrubbing floors, polishing cutlery – you should see the silver! Bet you're tired when you go to bed at night?'

'Yes, I'm exhausted! You too?'

'Exhausted! It's all that concentrating! And I miss everybody...'

'Me too... What's your bedroom like? How many people are you sharing with?'

And the two girls chattered happily all the way down to the Glenmiglo road-end, where Mairi and her babies, and Will and Davy were waiting for them. More ecstatic reunions and hugs all round, and then they all headed back up the hill for soup and bannocks with Jess.

Jess, careworn though she was, couldn't wait to see her little girls. It was a joyful occasion, having them all back home together. She wanted to know every detail of Beth's and Peggy's working arrangements, and living arrangements, and how well they had carried out their duties so far. Were their masters and mistresses content with their work? Were they fair and reasonable? Listening to her mother's detailed questions, Mairi realised that there were so many things which might have gone wrong for the girls, things that had never crossed her own mind. It was early days, but it seemed as if they had both landed well enough on their feet. Little Davy got bored, and interrupted the endless chatter about other people's households with an announcement, 'We've got a surprise, Beth and Peggy, and you don't know what it is!'

'What kind of a surprise?' Beth and Peggy wanted to know, and Davy and Will led them proudly outside and around the back of the cottage to show them two little pink piglets, snuffling among the acorns, under the giant oak. 'Ah, they're gorgeous!' trilled the girls, 'Where did we get them from?' Mairi coloured a little, but her mother said firmly, 'They were a gift from the big house. And a most welcome gift too. We won't go hungry next winter! We're very grateful, aren't we, Mairi?' and she cast a meaningful look at her oldest daughter. It seemed that whatever Mairi had done, or not done, in regard to the piglets, it was the right thing as far as Jess was concerned. No gift could have been more gratefully received, and at last, Mairi had done something right. There was less talk of how on earth the babies were to be fed when Mairi's milk ran out. Mairi didn't really know what to make of it; it felt as if other people were controlling her, making decisions all around her, and she would be the last one expected to have an opinion. Her mother seemed to imply that this was what she deserved, for having allowed herself to get pregnant in the first place. It was all bewildering. If only Jean-Luc would come home soon.

'Mother,' said Beth, 'did you know that the blacksmith's wife from Flegg is a good friend of Agnes, the factor's housekeeper?'

'What, Kate? Arthur, the blacksmith's wife? No, I didn't,' said Jess, 'but it doesn't surprise me,' she said, her voice sharpening. 'Makes sure she has friends in all the right places, that one. How did you find that out?'

'She came for a visit, when her husband was bringing back a cart he had repaired. When she found out who I was, she was asking after you, Mairi.'

'Me?' said Mairi, 'I don't think I know her at all.'

'It was something about a horse being stolen, she seemed to think you would know about it. They suspect that Jean-Luc who was working here – you know the one,' and she glanced at Peggy, 'the one who chased our Father that day...' Mairi opened her mouth in protest, but Beth continued with her story. 'She said that Jean-Luc had stolen a horse and then was seen riding for St Andrews. They think he was going back to France.'

Mairi gasped and then fell silent. She refused to meet her mother's eyes. Her heart was sore; but she had to keep things happy for her sisters' visit. Later on, she would take time to think about it. Jess spoke sharply to Beth, 'If that woman comes visiting again, make sure you tell her nothing. And you'd better be careful with that Agnes as well – she's probably gossiping about all of us. Having a field day.'

Beth and Peggy looked at each other – something for them to discuss on the long walk back. Then they brought out some gifts, sent by the new employers with best wishes.

Some cheese from the dairy at Nine Bells, and a bag of meal from the factor's kitchen. You could see the satisfaction on Jess's face, for once not being solely responsible for putting food on the table for her large family. 'Thank the ladies most kindly,' she ordered her twins. 'Tell them your mother is very pleased that you've settled down so well and is grateful for their mindings.'

All too soon it was time for Beth and Peggy to return up the Strath. Mairi's twins were hungry, and so it was decided that Jess would walk down with them to the road end, the boys skipping along in attendance, while Mairi fed the twins. This was a disappointment to Mairi; however, her own babies needed her and there was nothing else for it. Her mother could mind them, but not feed them. Her sisters were the ones out on the grand adventure; she had made her bed and must bide in it, as her mother often told her. She bid Beth and Peggy an affectionate farewell and settled down quietly for the long, slow feed.

So unusual to be alone in the house. She lit a candle against the gloaming, and settled back quietly, one twin under each arm, the little feet pointing out on either side, and then latching their open mouths firmly onto her firm, full breasts. Her own feet up on a stool. Soon the twins were sucking to a steady rhythm, soothing and almost hypnotic. She felt her own goodness being drawn out through her to fulfil the next generation. Through the window there was the flush of a red sunset. The candle spilled its golden light, and everything shimmered.

Mairi's eye caught a little pile of metal letters which Johnny and Davy had brought in from up the hill. They had left them next to the candle. Adjusting herself so as not to disturb the babies, Mairi reached over and took them in her hand. She fingered them gently. It would be good if she could read them, she considered. Like the monks. Like Jean-Luc as well, she remembered, wishing she could write to him, as he had written to her. How had he learned to read, she pondered? As she caressed the letters, they began to warm up – in fact, they were almost quivering. How strange.

In the somnolent evening air, with the steady sucking of the babies at her breast, a vision swam into Mairi's awareness; a girl with long red hair, sitting on top of a tall black horse. The girl was waving at her. Who could she be? The blacksmith's wife had spoken of a tall black horse, and suggested that Jean-Luc had stolen it – for all Mairi knew, maybe he had. Maybe he was in a hurry to get away, she thought, sadly. So, who was this girl? As the twins sucked gently at her, their first hunger assuaged, Mairi with half-closed eyes gazed into the green eyes of the girl on the horse. She was just a young thing, dressed very strangely, more like a boy really. The family resemblance was striking – she could almost have been Beth or Peggy, with the same cheeky look about her. The horse was turning round and preparing to canter away; the girl looked back over her shoulder, waved at Mairi and blew her a kiss – and then was gone. The vision faded.

What was the meaning of it? Both twins were slackening off from their feeding now. They had had enough. They were content; and so was she. This had been a thrilling moment, this visitation from some faraway friend. Not a love rival, she could tell – more likely a relation. Maybe a relation from the future? Yet to be born? Mairi frowned in bewilderment. What had come over her, thinking such things? She replaced the little letters carefully on the ledge by the candle, resolving to have a closer look at them again tomorrow, in daylight. She rose to her feet, a baby on each shoulder, and walked round the kitchen with them, patting their backs as well as she could without dropping either of them. Soon after, Jess and the boys came home, and Jess took little Archie off her. In another ten minutes, both babies were burped and cleaned and ready for night time. Jess was breezy, 'Well,' she said, 'that all seems to have gone very well, don't you think? My girls are doing just fine.' And she went outside to shut the hens in for the night.

Mairi was rinsing the babies' napkins out at the burn when she heard the beating of hooves on the path below. Her heart lurched and she ran to see who was coming. It was nearly dark now, with a full golden moon, and she stepped back as the horse and its rider came into view. Not a big black horse – a small bay, and the silhouette of the rider was not the strong bear-like form of the young Frenchman. The horse saw Mairi and reared up, and the rider pulled him to a halt. Leaning down, a man's voice enquired, 'Miss Mairi – what are you doing out at this time of night? Is all well?' Mairi recognised Brother Joseph from up the hill – gone, these last few months.

'Sir!' She spoke, her heart beating, 'You are riding alone?'

'Alone? Yes, of course,' he said, 'Just back from France. A good night to you.' And he urged the horse to trot on.

Mairi felt she was casting around in the dark. Nothing to pin her hopes to. Brother Joseph and Jean-Luc must have passed like ships in the night, one unaware of the other's direction. What was Jean-Luc up to? And would she ever see him again? Introduce Archie and Fiona to their father?

There was a squeak and snuffle from the piglets' pen. Mairi wandered round to pet them a little. That was another problem, she reflected, scratching their little noses. How should she respond to the young Douglas when he next came calling – as no doubt he would?

CHAPTER TEN

It was staff appraisal time at work. It was supposed to happen every year, but for various reasons it was nearer two years since the last time they'd all had to go through this. Ruth was dreading it; she found it excruciating to sit in a small room with her boss, going through her work performance with a fine-tooth comb. Even though Annabel, the vet, said it was all about personal development, and opportunities, and not about any kind of disciplinary matter – not that there would be anyway, with the standard of Ruth's work, her boss assured her – Ruth couldn't wait for it all to be over so that she could escape back to the pups and cats and budgies. Her mobile rang. She glanced at the screen. 'Do you mind if I take this, Annabel, it'll be quick,' she said. It was Wilson at the garage. Just to let her know they hadn't forgotten about her car, but were waiting for a part to come in. Out of stock for most suppliers, he explained, being so out of date... Ruth thanked him. Nothing for it now but to get on with the appraisal; get it over with.

There were two veterinary nurses in the practice, and Ruth was an animal care assistant – the only one. She usually ended up doing all kinds of odd jobs, with no two days the same, and that was what made the job so interesting for her. For somebody who had left school with hardly any qualifications, she felt she was lucky to have found such interesting work, right on her doorstep. No need to trek away to town every day, having to wear skirts and tights and make up. No need to sit and watch the clock and be bored beyond belief, as some of her friends had been in jobs in the past. Yes, she thought she was lucky. It never occurred to her that the vet's practice might be lucky to have her. She didn't see it that way at all. She was in awe of the two vet nurses, and as for the vet herself, as far as Ruth was concerned, Annabel was right up there with God, the Queen, and Freddy Mercury.

She had asked the nurses how they had got on with their own appraisals, to try and get a clue as to how it might work out; but they'd just shrugged and said it was fine, there was nothing to worry about. 'It's all about you and how you feel here, about your job.' This was of no comfort to Ruth at all. She had bought buns at the bakers, to try and convert the meeting into a social occasion; but it looked like the vet wasn't going to be so easily diverted.

'So, there are some new regulations coming in, Ruth, as we talked about before. Basically, they want everybody to have qualifications of some kind.'

'I don't have any qualifications though,' said Ruth, 'does that mean I'll be out of a job?'

'Not at all, you just need to do some training.'

Ruth fidgeted. She couldn't do training; the very idea.

'How long will my job last, without qualifications?' she asked.

'It's not about being out of a job, Ruth' insisted Annabel, 'Will you just listen to me? It's just that the government wants everybody to have qualifications nowadays. So that we are all singing from the same hymn sheet. So that we can all do our jobs better.'

'But I just have to ask you, or one of the others, if I need to know anything,' said Ruth, 'and I think I know most of the things I need to know anyway, for my job, don't I? Have I done something I shouldn't have done? Have I made some mistake or something? Has someone complained about me?'

'You do a superb job Ruth, how often do I have to tell you? But just doing a good job isn't enough on its own nowadays. You're going to have to do a course. There's nothing else for it. You don't need to be so nervous about it, it'll be quite interesting, really. You'll enjoy it.'

Ruth remained unconvinced, and staggered out at the end of the session clutching a leaflet about veterinary care assistant training. She had promised to look into it, and get back to Annabel in a day or two. As she walked home that night, she peered in the post office window to see if anybody needed any unskilled jobs doing. Or there was the possibility of the dog walking business of course, surely she wouldn't need to get qualifications to do that?

After tea that night, her phone rang; it was Kate, Jade's foster carer. They chatted for a while, trying to arrange a play date in some kind of nice place where the girls could run around while they had a coffee. 'Not that they want to play, as such,' Kate added. 'Is Morven the same? Getting too sophisticated for their own good. Jade's just a wee girl under-neath it all, but she pretends to be all grown up.'

'I know. It's a worry,' Ruth agreed. She and Kate had only got to know each other after the girls had been approached by a perv in a car park. Morven and Jade liked to meet up; they could talk to each other about things they didn't want anyone else to know about. And it was much the same for Ruth and Kate. Ruth confessed that the car was still in the garage. 'I had a call from them today – they can't get the part I need, it's such an old rust-bucket. I'm dreading them telling me it's not fixable, or else too expensive to fix.'

'Oh no,' said Kate, 'what would you do?'

'I don't know,' said Ruth, 'I'm absolutely stony broke.'

'Why don't you think about fostering?' said Kate.

'Well,' said Ruth, 'Astrid is doing some kind of assess-ment-thing at present for me to look after Morven. I don't think it's called fostering, I think it's kinship something. For your own family.'

'That's not what I meant,' said Kate, 'I meant what I do. You know, looking after other people's children.'

'I do that already, with Morven,' said Ruth.

'Yes, but complete strangers,' said Kate, 'Like I do.'

'I couldn't possibly do that,' said Ruth, 'I couldn't go through all that questioning and everything. What a nightmare!'

'It's not all that bad,' said Kate, 'they make it easy for you. It's not as if they need you to be all clever and academic or anything. You just need to be yourself – you know, sensible and practical. Good sense of humour! Anyway, it's very well paid – as well as getting an allowance to look after the kids, you also get a pretty good wage. That's how we can run two cars. It's not that we do it for the money, of course, but it helps.'

'Really?' said Ruth, 'That doesn't seem fair.'

'Well, I don't know about that,' said Kate. 'It's a hard job.'

'Yes, I know, that's not what I meant,' said Ruth. 'What I mean is, Astrid has told me how much I'll get if they approve me as a kinship person, and you could never describe it as a good salary. It's a pittance, in fact. It'll barely keep Morven in school shoes.'

'Well, what you're doing for Morven is very much the same as what I do for Jade. You should ask Astrid about it. You're right, it's not fair. I suppose they just take you for granted because you're her great-aunt.'

They chatted on for a while and agreed that Kate would pick her and Morven up at the weekend and they would check out the zipwires at a park on the road to St Andrews, just to ring the changes, and Ruth hung up and got the ironing basket out. She brooded over the rates of pay which Kate had mentioned. It was astonishing. She poured herself a glass of wine and kept ironing. She made supper for Morven, checked the homework, and made sure she got showered and into bed on time. The more she thought about it, the most resentful she felt. Here she was, being badgered at work to do some qualification which she knew she wouldn't be able to do, and at the same time taking good care of her great niece, a job that was undeniably difficult – and she couldn't even afford to have her car fixed. And yet there was Kate, doing exactly the same thing, and running two cars! Yes, she should certainly discuss it with Astrid.

Why not right now? She poured herself a second glass of wine, switched on her laptop and rattled off an email:

Dear Astrid, just wondering when the kinship money is coming through. Also wondering whether I shouldn't just apply to be a foster carer since it pays so much better. You keep telling me I'm doing a great job. Let's talk about it next time. Cheers, Ruth.

SHE KNEW ASTRID WAS VERY THOROUGH, ALBEIT IRRITATING and pedantic. She had experienced Astrid being condescending, bossy, and inflexible. But she had never known her to be angry – and when the phone call came next lunchtime, just as she was sitting down in the staffroom with her cheese sandwich and mug of tea, she realised that that was exactly what was different about Astrid's voice. But why?

'Is it all about money after all?' Astrid was saying, her voice icy. 'Of course you can't be a foster carer, however do you think you could keep Morven safe and secure with another child in the house, for goodness' sake? You must surely have realised that would be a very destructive thing for Morven? And anyway, you don't have a spare room, do you? If you want to take in other people's children then I would have to take Morven away, there's nothing else to be said. I just wouldn't put her through it, and I'm amazed that you have even considered it.'

'What?' said Ruth, baffled. 'Take her away? Over my dead body! Anyway, I didn't mean other children, I meant fostering Morven, like Kate does with Jade.'

'That's completely different!'

'I don't see why, it seems to be the same job. Anyway, I'm at work, surely this isn't the best time for this conversation?'

'I would have thought any time would be the best time to discuss Morven – isn't she your top priority after all? I'm very disappointed, Ruth. I'll call in on Friday. Bye for now.' And she put the phone down.

Suddenly the cheese sandwich and mug of tea had lost their appeal. Ruth sat there in shock, wondering what on earth she had said that could have angered Astrid so much. Take Morven away? *Take her away*? Ruth's blood ran cold at the very thought. She would have to deal with this straight-away. She picked up her phone and hit the return button. Couldn't let this lie.

But there was no reply. Ruth tried the office landline number; the receptionist said Astrid was out at a case confer-ence. 'Do you want to leave a message?'

'Ask her who the... who the... who she thinks she is, threatening to take Morven away from me!'

'Uh huh?'

Ruth was hot and breathing hard. Annabel had just come out of the prep room and was staring at her, aston-ished. What was she doing? Was this really going to help? 'No, cancel that,' she said. 'Better not. Just say I called. Thanks.'

'She'll call you back I expect.'

'Okay. Cheers.' Ruth burned with fury. She caught Annabel's eye. 'That's why I'm the wrong person to send on training,' she spat, and headed off to the loo.

CHAPTER ELEVEN

It was Shrove Tuesday up Glenmiglo Hill. The last day for gathering up and celebrating the little luxuries of life before Ash Wednesday and the long season of Lent. In Brother Joseph's absence, the religious observances had relaxed somewhat; neither Rodriguez nor Anselm being all that bothered, now that they were in hiding and officially no longer monks. 'We all took vows,' was Joseph's view. He insisted on the proper observation of Lent, with a ceremonious show of repentance and a return to the important things in life. The nights were dark, the wind bitterly cold – it was hard to believe that Spring might be just around the corner. The climate suited the forthcoming season of self-denial.

Today, however, after the Pancake Bell and confessions, there was an expectation of casual merriment. Jess planned to get most of her preparation done before the bell so that she could go off, confess her sins, and then get peace to finish things.

Before the sun was long up, she had cleaned out the Big House kitchen larder, washing down all the shelves, and set out the little frivolities for Lady Janet's modest family feast tonight; and some for the servants' hall. And there would also be a little pannier of dainties for Jess to take home to her own family. Eggs (for creation) and milk (for purity) were in short supply, since the cows didn't produce so much milk in the winter, and the hens slowed down their laying. However, by the end of Lent the days would have lengthened and the fertile season would be underway again, and so it was a good time to check on last year's oversupply of cheeses and hams.

She heaved a whole cheese up from the cellar, and when the kitchen maid had scrubbed the rinds down and cut out the little bits of mould, there was an ample supply for the big house including the servants, and Jess's home. She cut down the second last ham hanging from the rafters and cut away generous slices for the evening repast. There was plenty beremeal in the kist – the staff of life. Jess used the last of the precious soft wheat flour, mixed in with a pound of the bere-meal, a few eggs, and two quarts of milk, and some salt for wholesomeness; and mixed the batter in a large basin. This was best done first thing in the morning, ready for pouring into pancakes later that night. Next year, she reflected, they would have their very own hams to enjoy, perhaps keeping one pig for fattening up for next season. It would be a marvellous thing, she reflected, if they could replace a piglet each year so that they would always have a mature pig for slaughter, without depleting their store entirely. This would be something to discuss with Mairi, she decided. Although it might be something she should mention in confession. Not that Brother Joseph would have the faintest understanding of the problems she faced. And if the young Douglas was so disposed, what harm was there? She crossed herself over the pancake batter and covered the wide bowl with a cloth. Life was too complicated. Mairi had made it that way. Jess just wanted to survive.

As she was washing the wooden spoons, she heard hoof-beats in the backyard. Idly, she wondered who might be visiting on such a day – and her curiosity was satisfied a few minutes later when a head and shoulder were thrust around the kitchen door. To her surprise, it was the young Douglas. She jumped a little and, quickly recovering, dropped a curtsy. 'Good morning Sir,' she said, 'may I help you?'

'Good morning to you!' said the young man, bold as brass as Jess later remembered it. 'I was looking to see if the young lady was working this morning. Miss Mairi.'

'Miss Mairi is on the drying green Sir,' said Jess, hiding a smile. 'Just round the back to the left. And Sir,' she called, as the young Douglas turned to go, 'may I say how much we are enjoying your gift of the piglets.' And she bowed and curt-seyed again. The young man turned back, his face flickering in recognition.

'You are Miss Mairi's mother perhaps?' he said, 'Forgive me, I didn't recognise you from that terrible day at the quarry. I trust you are...' And he paused, too young and inex-perienced to know how to articulate what exactly he trusted for a woman widowed by a horrible accident, just over a year previously. Jess was similarly confused; neither of them quite knew what to say, so he bowed quickly and ran off in pursuit of the younger generation. Jess bit her lip and returned to the cleaning of the kitchen. Was Mairi still wearing that terrible old patched apron?

.   .   .

THE WASHING GREEN LAY OPEN TO THE SOUTH-WEST WINDS, ready to gather up the gusts that would blow everything fresh and dry. A small stand of birch trees between the big house and the green provided some shelter and privacy. In this way, the gentry didn't have to put up with the graceless-ness of their personal laundry flying in the wind; and the servants didn't have to feel overly observed as they went about their duties. Mairi had parked her babies, tightly wrapped in woollen shawls, in a little improvised pen made with a warm bundle of hay. They could sit up now unas-sisted, and gurgled at each other, finding great hilarity in their little world. They laughed and chuckled, and invented an entire universe for themselves, their mother safe nearby, and their little hands warmly tucked up in mittens. Mean-while, Mairi pegged out the blankets from the big house. There was a good fresh wind today, which would drive away the foulness of winter and bring a sense of spring into the bedchambers. Before leaving home that morning, Mairi had done exactly the same with their own blankets in the cottage. Mustn't waste a strong breeze.

So, blanket screens in place and Archie and Fiona duly occupied, Mairi set about pegging up the sheets, which she had scrubbed half an hour earlier. When she had finished this job, she planned to snuggle in the hay beside the babies, to feed them. Her breasts were tender and swollen, and she knew it would be time for their feed. Absorbed, she hauled up the last sheet and fixed it in place, the heavy linen flap-ping idly in the breeze. She removed her apron and arranged her woollen shawl around her shoulders, and was about to start unbuttoning her blouse, when she was surprised by the young Douglas stepping through the sheets. 'Good morning,' he cried, pulling off his hat and bowing from the waist. She was completely taken aback and laughed out loud, unable to help herself. A gentleman bowing at her? How silly. He laughed back at her. 'A fine day, is it not?' He saluted her.

'Indeed it is, Sir,' she said, pulling her shawl a little tighter around her shoulders.

'And how are my little piglets?'

Mairi froze. Was he referring to her babies? How dare he? What should she say? Then she remembered, with relief, that he was referring to his previous gift. How silly of her! 'They are delightful,' she laughed, 'My mother was so pleased.'

'Yes, I know,' said the young Douglas, 'I've just spoken to her.'

'Really?' said Mairi.

'I looked for you in the kitchen; she told me where to find you.' Mairi was astonished. Was her mother plotting? 'I have a little business with Sir Peter this morning,' said the young Douglas, 'but first I thought I would say hello to you.'

Mairi blushed, shrugged herself into her shawl and smiled awkwardly. She didn't know what to say. 'Your horse is lovely,' she said, 'such a fine sturdy neck. Did you have an early start this morning?'

'Not too early. My father's estate is just five miles away, up past Nine Bells.'

'Oh, quite nearby,' said Mairi, mentally taking note to find out from Beth and Peggy where the next estate up the Strath was situated.

'You can just about see my father's estate from the top end of Sir Peter's,' said the young man. 'Perhaps, Mairi, we could take a canter up there the next time I visit?'

Mairi's mouth fell open. 'Sir,' she started, wondering what to say next.

'Mairi, you must call me Richmond,' urged her suitor. His eye fell across her shoulder. 'I say!' he said, 'Whose are the babies?'

Mairi hesitated. She was tired of being judged. This, no doubt, would be a way of deterring this determined young man's advances. 'They're mine,' she said firmly, raising her chin.

'Really?' The young Douglas looked surprised, but only for an instant. 'You mean, your mother's?'

'Mine. My own. Last summer.'

'You're so young,' he murmured.

'Sixteen,' she replied.

'And are you... provided for?' he enquired.

Provided for? Mairi knew what he meant by this question. With all her heart she wanted to say yes! Their father is a most attentive provider! But, to her bitter regret, she could say no such thing. What to say, with confession coming up? 'My mother and I are grateful for Sir Peter and Lady Janet's ongoing patronage,' she said. 'My father's family worked here for many generations, and we hope this will continue to be the case.'

'Mairi, you amaze me,' said Douglas. 'You are a proud young woman, and I hope you will allow me to continue to visit you.'

She looked at him. There was no judgement in his eyes,

just appreciation and curiosity. She shook herself. 'Sir,' she started.

'Richmond!'

'Richmond, Sir – I really don't know what to say to you. You are kind to me. But I cannot reach beyond my station...'

'Don't worry, Mairi. If this were a different world, everything would be simple. But it's a complicated world. However,' and he smiled, 'all will be well. Will you accept these,' he said, reaching into his pocket and coming out with two florins. 'One for each of your fine babes. What are their names?'

She blinked. Nobody ever wanted to hear their names. 'Fiona,' she said, 'and Archie.'

He approached the babies in their makeshift cradle playpen. He held one florin out to Fiona and the other to Archie. 'Here you are, my fine babes,' he said, 'I will give these to your mother for safe keeping.' They gurgled back at him, and he laughed and turned round and handed the two coins to Mairi. Then blowing her a kiss, he leapt back on his horse and galloped off.

Shaking a little, Mairi cooried down into the hay with her babies, drawing her shawl around herself with the babies tucked inside, and settled herself for feeding. Whatever next? It was a strange world, right enough.

YOUNG RICHMOND DOUGLAS RODE ON UP THE HILL, BEYOND the farm buildings to where Sir Peter had arranged to meet him. Sir Peter and Joseph, who was sparing half an hour before preparing to take confessions, stood together at the foot of the fledgling orchard, considering its development.

They looked up at the drumming of hooves and stepped back to allow the young man to dismount and bow. Sir Peter turned to Joseph: 'I think you know our kinsman, Richmond Douglas?'

'Indeed,' said Joseph. 'Greetings, Sir.'

'We're just having a look at our new orchard,' said Sir Peter. 'Come and see! We were very pleased with our first harvest of plums last year, but the apples and pears didn't give us much. By God's grace, it will be better this year.'

'I'm most impressed Sir,' said Douglas. 'We have nothing like it up our hill. Is the hillside a suitable site for an orchard? North-facing, isn't it?' He addressed this to Joseph.

'I will introduce you to my colleague Rodriguez,' said Joseph, 'if you would like to know more. He is the one who knows best about the orchards. However, I can say that this is land which was never very productive for barley, so fruit trees make good use of it. In the autumn, with the windfalls, we found it was ideal for letting the pigs wander through. And get fattened up.'

'Is your father thinking of planting an orchard, Richmond?' said Sir Peter.

'Well, that isn't why I came here today, as you know, Uncle. But we are always interested to see different ways of doing things.'

'Joseph is going to produce a book, to explain to landowners how to establish the orchards – aren't you, Joseph?'

'A book?'

'Well yes, but it's early days...'

'In any case, Joseph,' said Sir Peter, 'to get back to Douglas's principal purpose in visiting here today.'

'Yes?'

'Let me explain,' said the young Douglas, 'I am to be married before long to my cousin, who lives the other side of Dundee. My parents and I hope most sincerely that you will conduct the ceremony; she too is loyal to the Queen and to the Roman faith, and so we would like to marry in that tradition. We wondered if you would be willing to make the journey to Arbroath to bless our union?'

'Care will have to be taken,' replied Joseph, 'but we must not allow the reformers' men to drive us away from the God-given ways.' So, the three men turned towards the big house to discuss the details. Within half an hour, it was all agreed, to take place the week after Easter. As the satisfied young Douglas rode up the hill afterwards, the Pancake Bell rang out for confessions.

Suitably shriven, Sir Peter mentioned his conversation with their nephew to Lady Janet at luncheon, and Lady Janet went quickly to the kitchen afterwards to speak to Jess.

'It's as I expected,' said Lady Janet, 'I understand it's a marriage of convenience; no doubt leaving him unsatisfied in certain respects.'

'It's nothing new,' replied Jess, 'Not what I would have hoped for, for my oldest daughter, but in the circumstances...'

'Mairi is a clever girl. Her life isn't over yet,' said Lady Janet, 'and I think young Douglas is a good man. I doubt he would mishandle her. I have always been very fond of his mother and father.'

Jess poured the first ladleful of pancake mix onto a

heated girdle, and spread it out with the back of the ladle. 'Well, she can't afford to be choosy, Ma'am. I thank you for your understanding. Let's just see how it goes.'

Mairi walked back down the hill with her babies. She had seen young Douglas galloping past half an hour before, and wondered idly what his business with Sir Peter had been. She was wondering what she would tell Jean-Luc when he returned, about the piglets, and the florins. That was going to be tricky. But really, she concluded, where was Jean-Luc when his children needed florins? Or when she needed piglets? He would have to understand that he had left her with very few choices in life. How was she to bring their babies up otherwise?

And, being an honest girl, she was aware also of a little frisson of excitement in her heart at being the object of admiration for once. She remembered that night, tumbling in the hay with Jean-Luc. It had been such an unexpected excitement, and she caught her breath as she remembered the thrill and the tremor of it all. What if she never had that thrill again? What if it took Jean-Luc so long to return, that she was too old to enjoy it?

What were her alternatives? Rejecting Richmond Douglas's overtures, given his persistence, would be difficult: for one thing, her mother would be outraged. And secondly, how on earth do you refuse someone when the balance of power and privilege is so decidedly in the other person's favour? And third – there was no denying it – the whole thing was rather exciting, and if it hadn't been for the tricky business of explaining it to Jean-Luc, she would have been all for it. She imagined telling Beth and Peggy about it – what would they say? She laughed out loud at the prospect.

She climbed over the stile, holding her babies tight to her chest. They were getting heavier now, and less easy to tuck under her arm and run along. It wouldn't get any easier as the years passed by, as she was well aware.

Jess had got home before her. She turned as her daughter came in and said, without preamble, 'Young Douglas is to be wed after Easter.'

'Wed?' said Mairi in consternation, her shoulders dropping. 'Wed? Does that make me a whore?'

CHAPTER TWELVE

Aunt Linda was coming down from Arbroath for the weekend. The planned day visit, over the course of a couple of telephone conversations, ended up being extended to the full weekend. Since neither Linda nor Ruth had transport, it seemed only sensible to make good use of the lengthy bus journey. Aunt Linda had a bus pass, so it wasn't costing her anything; and she wouldn't hear of Ruth coming to meet her in Kinbuckie, where she would have to change buses. 'I'll be fine,' she insisted, 'don't forget I grew up in Flegg, even though it's been a while. I know my way around.'

Ruth had aired the spare bedding and reorganised things so that Linda would have a room of her own. There was no spare room in her little house, so she put up a camp bed in Morven's room, so she and Morven would share for two nights. 'Are you okay with this?' she asked more than a few times; and Morven just shrugged. She didn't mind at all. For most of her life, her sleeping arrangements had been chaotic. She certainly enjoyed her own room with a clean bed and her pictures on the walls; but she was perfectly happy to share for two nights. Especially since it meant they'd get to see her new Aunt Linda. 'Why don't you let Aunt Linda share with me?' she asked Ruth, 'And then you could stay in your own bed.'

'Well, I thought about that,' said her Aunt, 'but I think it would be only polite to give our guest a room to herself.' Ruth was also a little anxious about Astrid's excessive attitude to risk assessment.

'Okay then,' said Morven, 'no problem.' She made a mental note to herself to make sure there was nothing lying around that she didn't want Aunt Ruth to see.

Her own preparation for Aunt Linda's visit was indirect – it didn't really involve Aunt Linda at all, but she had to dispose of all her stock before that weekend, in case Ruth found it and started asking questions. Morven, having decided that she had no other options, had set up her shoplifting operations with care. She didn't want to be found out and go through all the humiliation that would entail; it had been bad enough when her mother was alive. She had discovered that, since there were plenty shops in Kinbuckie, where she now went to school, it was simple to steal small things from lots of different places, rather than always from the same shop – which made it easier not to get caught. So far, she had been 100% lucky, with an unbroken record. The Easter eggs were already on sale, and there was a ready playground market for cut-price cream eggs and foil-wrapped bunnies. Morven's method entailed paying for one small egg, to divert the shop assistant's attention away from the stolen ones she had slipped into her deep pockets. It was fairly straightforward with practice, and she incorporated it into her daily routine without much difficulty. Her goal was to plant £25 in Aunt Ruth's purse before Aunt Linda's visit, to help pay for all the little extras. She had heard Ruth on the phone, ordering a free-range chicken at the butcher's, well beyond her usual food budget. Morven was up to £21.50, with just a few hours to go.

There was a girl in second year who inspired a certain amount of fear among her peer group. She seemed to have a way of making people do things they didn't want to do, with various methods of enforcing her wishes. Her name was Charlene MacTell, and everybody was scared of her. Except for Morven, of course. She wasn't really scared of bullies, having learned how to duck and dive among a whole range of scary characters while her mother was alive, but she was cautious about getting involved with that crowd. Well, maybe she was scared of them after all. Her rescue by Aunt Ruth was still too recent for complacency. She didn't want to go back down that slippery path. However, when Charlene MacTell offered her a fiver for one of the big hand-decorated chocolate eggs in the specialist Chocolatier in the High Street, Morven decided she would rise to the challenge. 'Six-Fifty and it's yours,' she heard herself saying, to her own astonishment.

It took a lot of planning; it was a different matter entirely, stealing something that size compared to grabbing a couple of cream eggs in the passing. There were two strategies to consider – first, she had to locate the CCTV camera and make sure she was blocking its view; and second, she wanted to ensure that the shop assistant's attention was otherwise diverted when she was in the act. The first part was straightforward. In terms of the second part, distracting the shop assistant's attention, she considered asking Kyle to go into the shop with her and deliberately distract the woman. However, she didn't really want to implicate Kyle, who had no idea what she was doing. He would be affronted if they caught her with him helping. And Morven had a sneaky feeling that Kyle would feel the need to tell his Dad – who would probably then want to tell Aunt Ruth. So, she decided to wait until there was some other disruption going on in the shop and take advantage of that.

She chose the busiest part of the day, at lunchtime when the schools were out, and the shop packed. A gaggle of third-year girls from the Catholic high school were making a fuss over the special Valentine's Day promotions, and soon started asking the assistant about prices, and whether they could have their target boys' names piped onto the eggs, perhaps with special messages. There was a lot of giggling and jostling involved. This was perfect for Morven. Coolly, during this lively conversation, she slipped the giant egg that her customer wanted into her rucksack, keeping her back between the camera and the shelf; and then waited patiently in a queue behind the third-year girls, holding two little chocolate ducklings. She paid for them and left quietly, undisturbed by any discovery of theft on her part. Twenty minutes later she had met with Charlene MacTell in the school playground and exchanged the goods for six lovely pounds and fifty pence. So that was her sorted for Aunt Linda's visit.

The rest of the day went as per normal, with some fairly boring classes but nothing too unbearable. She got the bus home at the end of the day, arriving just half an hour before

Aunt Linda was due. While Aunt Ruth was making up the spare bed, Morven slipped the £25 into her purse, then went to get changed out of her school uniform. Nothing could be easier. She was very pleased with her results.

It was great to see Aunt Linda again. Ruth and Morven were waiting for her at the bus stop, and they all greeted each other fondly – it hardly felt as if they had been such strangers to each other until recently. 'But you must have remembered Aunt Linda from when you were little?' queried Morven.

'Well yes, up to a point,' said Ruth, 'I think she was just a few years older than my Mum, but I don't remember her staying in Flegg. She must have left home early.'

'We should ask her,' said Morven. 'Don't forget, you've got our family tree to research.'

A shadow flitted through Ruth's eyes. 'Yes, that's true. But don't be too nosy about it either, Morven, you never know, she may have things she doesn't want to talk about.'

'Such as?'

'I don't know, all sorts of things,' said Ruth. 'You know how it is.'

'Skeletons in the cupboard?'

'Where did you hear that expression?'

'I don't know. In English, I think. The teacher said it was an example of a metaphor.'

'What's a metaphor?'

'I don't know. But I know what a skeleton in the cupboard is.'

'Yeah so do I,' said Ruth grimly, 'we've got a few.'

Aunt Linda climbed off the bus a little stiffly. Ruth and Morven, waiting at the bus stop for her, were alert for the suggestion of skeletons in her cupboard, and noted the stiffness with surprise. 'How old is she?' whispered Morven but Ruth just motioned her to shush.

'Well! Things haven't changed much round here!' announced Linda as she looked around her.

'When did you leave Flegg, Aunt Linda?' asked Morven straight out, somewhat to Ruth's embarrassment. But Linda wasn't phased.

'1961,' she replied, 'before either of you were born. It's a long story. Let's get back to your place, I'm desperate for a cuppa.'

MORVEN TOOK AUNT LINDA'S WHEELY BAG, AND THEY SET OFF down towards the river and along the avenue. 'Oh yes, I remember this,' Aunt Linda was saying, 'What happened to the factory that stood here? Oh yes, I remember hearing about it – the fire...'

'That must have been after you left?'

'Years after. But it's been such a long time since I've been back here, and I'd forgotten what a bonnie wee town it is. What a view you have of the river! It's magnificent!'

They had pizza for tea, and Morven's two aunts shared a bottle of wine, with coke for Morven – a special-occasion treat. 'How did you get on with those letters?' Aunt Linda suddenly asked Morven. The question threw Morven a little; she didn't want to discuss the letters in front of Aunt Ruth, who wasn't tuned in to their magical powers. 'Oh yes, fine,' she said, avoiding eye contact, and racking her brains for a way to change the subject.

'Do they work for you, then?' asked Aunt Linda, passing a bowl of crisps. 'According to my sister, Alison had the gift, but I never did.'

'What gift?' Aunt Ruth was refilling the glasses. 'Morven, would you like some more coke?'

'Yes please,' said Morven, 'I'll get it.' And she grabbed her glass and ran out to the kitchen. She felt caught between her two aunts. She wanted to find out more about this mysterious gift, but she didn't think it would do Aunt Ruth any good to hear about it.

She stood at the living room doorway, leaning on the jamb, one foot ready to escape if it all became too difficult. 'Alison used to be able to communicate with previous generations through those letters,' announced Aunt Linda, relaxing back into her armchair, putting her slippered feet up on the stool.

'Did she?' Morven was enthralled.

'Apparently so. I never got to discuss it with her because I was in India when she was born. You too, Ruth, I missed both your births. I kind of regret that now; I suppose I could have been more helpful to my sister – your mother, Ruth. But I wanted to see the world. Flegg felt too small for me back then.'

'But what about the letters?' Morven wanted to know about the family history, but the question of the little metal letters was more urgent, especially if she wasn't the first in the family to discover their powers.

'Something to do with the Middle Ages I think,' Linda

looked at the young girl. 'You can do it too, can't you? I can see it in your eyes.'

Aunt Ruth's mouth was hanging open. Morven was acutely embarrassed. 'It's nothing to worry about,' continued Aunt Linda, 'just a little second sight kind of thing. Like I say, my sister Alison had it – though it never did her any good – but I never did. I think it probably passed down the female line, missing out a few generations on the way.'

'Second sight?' Aunt Ruth was repeating. 'Second sight? In our family?'

'I suppose it touches all sorts of families,' said Aunt Linda, 'I'm pretty chilled about it. People in other cultures are much more open to that sort of thing. So,' she said turning to Morven, 'how does it work for you?'

Morven was staring at her Aunt Ruth, trying to figure out how this conversation might end. 'Come on, just spit it out,' said Aunt Linda. 'Don't worry about it, Ruth, it's just one of the peculiar things about our family.'

'You mean, yet another peculiar thing about our family!' said Ruth.

'Whatever. Come on then Morven,' and she looked again at Morven, fixing her with those clear green eyes, and inviting her to chat quite normally about something which up till now, in Morven's eyes, had been anything but normal. On the other hand, as she knew, it hadn't scared her either; it just seemed to be something that was part of her.

'I didn't know there was anything about our family in all of this,' she started, 'I thought it was just me.'

'What are you talking about? What do you mean, *just me*?' asked Ruth – you could see her anxiety rising, despite Aunt Linda's reassurances.

'You know the labyrinth?' said Morven cautiously.

'Yes.' Aunt Ruth was putting her glass down on the coffee table and leaning forward. 'What about it?'

'When I buried my time capsule,' said Morven, 'somebody dug it up, somebody from long ago. A Frenchman.'

Recognition flickered in Aunt Ruth's eyes. Morven continued, 'He said he would help me out, and that he would be a strong friend. So, we write to each other from time to time.'

'Really?' said Aunt Linda excitedly. 'That's amazing!'

'Really?' Said Aunt Ruth, in horror. 'That's worrying!'

Morven decided to follow her Aunt Linda's train of thought, rather than her Aunt Ruth's – it was too late to start lying about it now. 'And when I hold the little letters, they heat up and vibrate, and then I see a woman with long flowing red hair, just like mine, only less frizzy, and she is smiling at me. The last time I saw her, after you gave me those new letters for the train, Aunt Linda, she had two little pink things in her arms. 'I thought at first piglets; and then maybe babies.'

'Who do you think she is?' Aunt Ruth directed the question at Linda.

Aunt Linda was excited. 'That's the same woman that Alison used to talk about,' she said, 'and Alison thought she was our great great-great great-something grandmother!'

'That's exactly what I thought too,' said Morven. She turned to Aunt Ruth. 'Remember the drawing I put at the top of the family tree?' And she jumped to her feet. 'Come on and I'll show you, Aunt Linda,' she said.

They spent the next hour on the stairs, as Morven explained the portraits on her family tree to her Aunt Linda, with Ruth filling in the detail that she had gleaned from her genealogical searches. Aunt Linda was fascinated; having travelled all her life, she had missed out on the more recent events in the family – in particular, she had been unaware that her sister Alison's daughter, Aileen, had become so hopelessly involved in drugs. 'I wish I'd known about this at the time,' she said repeatedly, 'if only I could have helped you both! I feel so bad for you.'

'Don't feel bad,' said Ruth. 'It never occurred to me to look for family help. I wasn't even aware you were still alive.'

'But you've had such a terrible time!' said Aunt Linda. 'Morven, you poor wee soul!' And she put her arms round Morven's thin shoulders to attempt a hug which Morven more or less accepted before shrugging away.

'What interests me,' said Ruth, putting the issue of Morven and the Frenchman aside for the moment, 'was why Aileen's Mum, my sister Alison, wasn't a better parent to Aileen. Aileen seems to have been hurt somehow, and I can't imagine how that could have happened in our family.'

'Alison wasn't born when I left Flegg,' said Aunt Linda. 'I can see I need to search my memory a bit. I probably didn't pay enough attention to letters from home. Or maybe they didn't tell me... I thought I could get away from it all...'

The mood had dipped somewhat; all three women were feeling the shivers of past events. 'Let's get the kettle on,' said Aunt Ruth, 'it's your bedtime Morven. We've plenty of time for talking over the weekend.'

'What are we doing tomorrow?' asked Linda.

'Well,' said Ruth, 'if the weather continues fair, I thought we'd take a walk along the coastal path. But first thing, before that, I have to get up to the butchers to collect a chicken.'

'Lovely,' said Linda.

'Lovely,' echoed Morven, wondering if her aunt had looked in her purse yet. This weekend had taken an unexpected turn, and it was only Friday night! It seemed like the intrigue was only just beginning.

CHAPTER THIRTEEN

As the pinched season of Lent wore its way across the Flegg countryside, many travellers appeared from upriver, travelling eastward. Some of them came to the cottage door seeking food or rest. If Jess was at home, she sent them straight up to the Big House. 'Pilgrims!' she would sniff, 'Beggars, more like!'

Mairi wondered what it would be like to go on a pilgrimage. She had heard tell of pilgrims crossing Scotland on their way to St Andrews – some had travelled hundreds of miles to get there; and as far as she was aware, St Andrews was just around the corner from Glenmiglo, a half-day horse's gallop away; and yet, completely out of her reach. Nobody of her acquaintance had ever been there. Even her little sisters, now in service at estates within five miles' distance, had travelled further than Mairi had in her lifetime. What was a pilgrim anyway?

She had a chance to find out. One morning, a few days later, she was sweeping the floor in the Great Hall. Anselm, the most approachable of the monks, was meeting with Sir Peter, and sneezed at the cloud of dust being raised by the servant girl.

He blinked in surprise at being addressed directly. 'Forgive me, Brother, but I hear tell of many pilgrims coming up the Strath these days. And I don't even know what a pilgrim is. Can you help me?'

Brother Anselm paused. 'An interesting question! Pilgrims are seeking a restoration, or a healing, of the body – or perhaps of the mind.'

'Healing? And they get that by walking long distances?'

'So it seems.' Anselm settled into a comfortable position, leaning on his stick. 'I have met many pilgrims who swear to have come to terms with dreadful misfortunes, or to have found inspiration for important changes they must make in their lives. It's the discomfort, you know, and the lack of familiarity; being taken away from your own bed, or your own fireside. It gives you a chance to think along different lines. Perhaps to recognise past mistakes, or to shine a light on one's future path.'

'Perhaps it works best for people who have comfortable home lives then,' said Mairi, shrugging. 'I think it must only be rich people who go on pilgrimages.'

'You may be right, my dear,' said Anselm. 'Although sometimes also, people who have done something illegal, or immoral, in their own country are sent to walk on a long pilgrimage, to wash away their sins. To repent.'

'Instead of being sent to the dungeon?' said Mairi.

'Well, sort of. It's not necessarily a punishment, more a penance.'

Sins? Penance? Mairi decided to drop the subject before

it turned personal. 'Forgive me Brother, I mustn't hold you back. I just wondered about all these travellers.'

'They may be pilgrims,' said Anselm, 'or they could be refugees. All these persecutions, in the church's name, God forgive us ... And also we hear tell of the Plague lingering on. Many of the travellers through these parts, I believe, are on their way to St Andrews.'

'Bound for France?'

'Possibly. Or else just on their journey. Who knows where? For any of us?'

And that night, feet up on the stool feeding Fiona and Archie, she wondered about her own life's journey. Should she be repenting? It seemed that everyone thought her a rank sinner, for having conceived her beautiful babies in such a casual way. Or in a way which they, knowing absolutely nothing at all about the situation, considered casual. Mairi did not consider herself a sinner in this respect. The getting of the babies had been a wonderful experience, and one which she hoped to repeat over and over again – though not necessarily always resulting in babies if it could be helped – and lead to lifelong happiness with their father. If he came back.

Accepting gifts from the young Douglas, who was about to marry a woman of his own class, was a different matter, however. She would have to think this one through. It seemed that if you were rich, then you could arrange things to suit yourself. Nobody seemed to dismiss Richmond Douglas as a sinner. And if you weren't rich, but you were a man, you could still make your own decisions, choose your own directions. Like her father – a crabbit old bastard whom she wouldn't forgive, sustained by the endless toils of his wife and family, and ungrateful at every stage. Wasn't he a sinner? Was he ever expected to repent? Quite the opposite – Sir Peter obviously regarded him as the true tenant of the cottage, leaving her and her mother and the other children in jeopardy after his untimely death.

Then again, there was Jean-Luc – not a rich man, but somehow separated from his family and brought to Scotland, and now sent away for his presumed part in her father's death. Without evidence or trial, even though it was fairly obvious what had happened. But Jean-Luc was free to travel around as he chose. That night in the barn was a joint delight, something not planned but freely given and received on both sides with joy. But she was left with the babies, not him, and she didn't suppose anyone criticised him or expected him to repent.

Sin. What was it, exactly? Slippery. More prevalent for some people than others, like women and poor people. Not rich men. She sighed. It felt heavy to be judged as sinful.

Then again, there were the monks – good men, as far as she could see – not rich, but with all that education. They were clever, they could read and write. How useful would that be? If she could write, she thought, maybe she could send a letter to Jean-Luc. Or even write to Richmond Douglas, and demand an explanation of his intentions. Rather than just having to wait for him to turn up when it suited him – either before or after his wedding.

She remembered the occasion when Jean-Luc had written to her, and she had to beg Sir Peter and Brother Joseph to read the letter to her, and then she had to steal it from them to keep it. Her own letter! Why was it a privilege that some people had, and others didn't?

As the babies suckled on, she dozed a little. She had a dream of the young girl with the long red hair, last seen riding away on a big black horse. This time in her dream, Mairi saw the girl working on a great wide sheet of smooth white paper, with pencils – drawing a picture of somebody she was looking at. Concentrating. And as she finished the drawing, she was writing something along the bottom. Mairi squinted to see what it was, to make sense of the scrawl. Perhaps it was the name of the person whose picture she was drawing, or perhaps her own name. These would be interesting to see – how frustrating! If only she could read. She opened her eyes. Little Archie had stopped sucking and fallen asleep, his nose nuzzling into her armpit. Little Fiona had also finished feeding, and was staring at her with big blue eyes, just beginning to turn green. The reddening tinge of her soft, fine hair was unmistakable among the blonde. 'If I'm a pilgrim,' Mairi brooded, 'on a journey, I want to go to a place where I can understand things. Instead of understanding nothing. Maybe I could unravel all kinds of secrets. Why not? I'll just have to keep on asking questions.'

This was her journey – a mysterious route by which she would discover how to stop being pushed around by other people's whims; how to live her own life and live it well; how to be happy. How to make her babies and her sisters and brothers and her mother happy. How to stop people judging her. Or how to know when they were wrong, and she was right, and how to not let them bother her. And she would learn all this just by keeping on asking questions.

The first question she needed to ask, she decided, was

'how can I learn to read and write?' That was her job for the following day. Her candle was guttering; she checked Archie and Fiona; both fast asleep, content, beyond judgement. Time she went to sleep too. To be ready for her journey to begin.

CHAPTER FOURTEEN

The roast chicken had been fabulous. 'Which butcher did you go to?' Aunt Linda wanted to know. 'There used to be three butchers in Flegg...' This was boring adult talk and although Morven had enjoyed the chicken very much, she was just glad that it had kept Aunt Ruth from reverting to the Jean-Luc issue.

They took the dishes out to the kitchen and got started on the clean-up. It seemed as if they had used every dish in the house, whereas normally there was just a pile of plastic and cardboard wrappers to recycle, and a wipe around the microwave. But there was no question. Dinner had been great. It was worth stealing £25 to help put that kind of food on the table, she considered, and to have everyone feeling so contented.

Aunt Linda had stripped all the rest of the meat off the carcass, and put the bones in a big pot of water on top of the stove, to come to the boil. They were off again, still talking about the chicken. It was like being on Celebrity Master-

Chef. Fun, really, but there was a limit. Morven dried the last spoon and put it away, hung up her dish towel and said, 'Can I put the telly on?'

'Okay,' said Ruth, 'but first – have you got homework?'

'No.'

'You didn't even think about that!' said Ruth, 'Go and check your schoolbag.'

'But I could do it tomorrow after Aunt Linda goes away!'

'I'd like to see it,' said Aunt Linda. 'Go and look it out, and I'll see if I can help you with it.' Morven grudgingly nodded and disappeared upstairs to find her schoolbag.

'Linda,' began Ruth, 'there's something I need to ask you.'

'What's that?'

'Did you put money in my purse?'

'Money?'

'Yes – £25.'

'No, I didn't. I was going to offer you some later on. Why do you ask?'

'Oh, don't, Linda, please. It's just that a couple of times recently, I seem to have had more money in my purse than I expected.'

'Nice problem! Maybe you just counted wrong?'

'Maybe. But I don't think so. You sure you weren't just trying to help me out?' she said.

'No, that's not how I help people out,' said Aunt Linda. 'Not in secret like that, I'd have told you. Even though you wouldn't have wanted to accept anything.'

'I suppose so.'

There was a pause in the conversation while Linda chopped an onion for the soup. 'Do you need some money?'

'No. Thank you.' The two women were quiet for a moment.

'It's quite a lot of money to have not known about,' said Aunt Linda, 'where else might it have come from?'

Ruth looked at Linda, 'I'm just a bit concerned about Morven,' she began.

'Why is that?'

'In case she thinks she's trying to help me out. But then, where is she getting the money?'

'Have you asked her?'

'Not yet,' said Ruth, 'she would be really embarrassed if I raised anything like this in front of you. But I don't know what to do about it; it's really a worry.'

Morven hadn't reappeared after being sent for her schoolbag, and Ruth guessed that she had got absorbed in something else, and forgotten – or else was prevaricating about doing the homework at all. She was still upstairs, so Ruth quietly shared some of the experiences of the last year with Aunt Linda while they sat in the kitchen with a coffee.

'We still have to go to the Children's Panel every so often, but at least they've taken her off the 'At Risk' register. What a life she's had. That's why she's so small for her age – poor nutrition as a baby, and constantly moving house. I call it 'house', but you know, it was just squats. No wonder she's so immature, and yet she turns into a tiger when anything frightens her. We're not out of the woods yet, I don't think, her and me.'

'Just how skint are you?' asked Aunt Linda, in a common-sense voice. 'I mean, are you in debt or anything? Is there anybody you owe money to?'

'No! Honestly, thank goodness, no debt. All the bills are

paid. But to be honest, there isn't much left behind at the end of the week. I'm always desperate for payday.'

'Any chance of a pay rise?'

'Don't get me started on that one!' said Ruth. 'They want me to do some kind of qualification-thing, just to keep doing the same job, and I just know I won't to be able to do it. So, I will have to look for another job, and the chances of getting a job I like, in Flegg, which even paid the same as what I get now, never mind giving me a pay rise. I can't...'

'Let me stop you there a minute,' said Linda. 'Why won't you be able to do the qualification you're talking about? If you're doing the job already, anyway?'

'Well I could never be bothered when I was at school, and I wasted a lot of time, and there were always people cleverer than me, and ...'

'I suppose it wasn't important to you back then,' said Linda. 'Probably you hadn't ever had to juggle the cost of electricity bills and new school shoes and all the rest of it?'

'True, but...'

'Whereas now, it's obvious, isn't it?' said Linda.

'What is?'

'If you want to earn more money, you probably have to get this qualification. In fact, other qualifications too perhaps, that's the way of the world nowadays. It's all changed since I was a girl. But you're not a stupid woman Ruth, you can easily do this.' Ruth was staring at Linda in disbelief. 'Don't look at me like that! Just think of all the people you know who have passed an exam and got the odd promotion and end up earning more than you do – is it because they're cleverer than you?'

Ruth thought for a moment.

'Sometimes.'

'But not always?'

'Not always,' Ruth conceded.

'Absolutely. How do you expect Morven to stick in at the school and work hard, if you're not showing her that kind of example?'

Ruth gasped. She had never expected Linda to be so plainspoken – and she had never thought about it that way either. 'But it's just school! I'm not expecting her to be a genius! I just want her to get by!'

'I thought you wanted her to go to art school? In fact, I thought Morven herself wanted to go to art school?'

'Well yes, I know,' said Ruth in a small voice, 'but honestly? Art school? How could I support her through art school when I can hardly pay the mortgage at the end of the month?'

'So, you're giving up on her career before you've even begun?' Tears sprung to Ruth's eyes. 'I'm sorry if this seems harsh, Ruth, but honestly. You're a very able woman, and you just haven't given yourself the right challenge yet. You've done an incredible job turning Morven around to where she is now – and I know you say she's not there yet, but it sounds like she's so much further forward than she was, say, a year ago – and that's remarkable! Most people couldn't do that, as I'm sure you know. So just knuckling under and learning how to pass a few exams will be a walk in the park to you. Honestly, I mean it – believe me! You can do this.'

Ruth was silent, really taken aback. 'How did we get to this point?' she asked, suddenly feeling lame. 'We started off talking about Morven's homework, and here are you telling me I've got to go and do some qualifications?'

Linda held her eye. 'I think you know it makes sense, Ruth.'

'I'm too old.'

'How old are you?'

'Thirty-nine. Forty in September.'

'I'm seventy-three,' said Linda, 'and there's lots of life left in me yet. You've barely begun.'

Silence. 'Well – possibly. Let's leave it for now, maybe think about it again tomorrow,' Ruth replied.

Morven came back downstairs carrying her schoolbag. 'Aunt Linda,' she said, 'I have to do some drawings for school, can I draw you?' Ruth noted, with an unexpected pang of jealousy, how much more confident Morven was already about this. 'Draw me?' said Aunt Linda, 'Only if you let me draw you at the same time.'

'Don't be daft, that would never work,' said Morven, 'you have to keep still.'

'Well, you show me what to do – first you draw me, and then I'll draw you.' The two of them sat down at opposite ends of the sofa, with Aunt Linda trying different poses on, and making Morven giggle. They settled down quickly, with Morven concentrating hard to capture her new Aunt's features on paper. Ruth watched for a while and concluded she was glad that Linda had come into their lives. However, she hadn't expected such a forthright challenge. That smarted a lot.

She wondered if she had been too cowardly in dismissing the very idea of the vet care assistant training that Annabel had tried to coax her into. Maybe Aunt Linda was right – other people seemed to manage to do this sort of thing. She rummaged through her mind, and without even trying, came up with five names of people in the town who had gone back to college long after leaving school, and got themselves better jobs as a result. She knew she wasn't stupid; at school, she had been middle of the class, sometimes higher up. Right enough, she had never bothered about homework – there always seemed to be more interesting things to do after school. When she didn't understand where the rest of the class had got to in lessons, she had concluded that she just wasn't made for learning. She couldn't wait to leave school and get a job, and back then it was easy enough to get work. So much more satisfying, earning your own money! And then she'd met Gordon when she was only sixteen, fallen madly in love, and the two of them had got married the day after her 18th birthday. By that time, school was a distant memory.

With Morven and Linda fully engaged in their activity, Ruth rummaged in her handbag and brought out the leaflet that Annabel had given her the other day. Maybe time to have a proper look. At least it would keep her mind off the next issue to tackle with Morven – the mysterious £25 which had appeared in her purse from nowhere. She unfolded the leaflet. It didn't tell her the things she needed to know, like how much the course would cost, or where she would have to go for lessons. However, it listed some subjects that would be taught, all of which were familiar to Ruth. They were things she did every day: exercising, grooming and feeding, cleaning and preparing accommodation for animals, restraining animals for treatment and various other things like that. Surely it couldn't be that simple? There was a mention of maths and English, which made her bite her lip. She looked up at Aunt Linda and Morven still contentedly scribbling away at their drawings. What difference would it make to their lives if she suddenly had to start bringing homework back with her?

It was already dark, and she'd drawn the blinds when there was a ring at the doorbell. Ruth went to the door to see who it was at this time of night. A child she recognised from further up the town was standing hunched on the doorstep, hands in pockets, jacket hood up. 'Is Morven in?' the girl asked.

'Do I know you?'

'Angela Higgins. Is Morven in?'

'It's getting late.' But Morven had come through to the hallway to see who was speaking and flinched when she saw Angela. 'What is it?' she addressed Angela, her chin up.

Ruth stood back a bit, wondering what was going on.

'Get me one of those big eggs,' said the girl. 'I need it for next Friday, right? With MUM in pink writing on it.' And she turned on her heel and marched off. Morven looked shocked and then made to run after Angela, but Ruth pulled her back and slammed the door. 'Okay Morven,' said Ruth, 'level with me. What was all that about?'

'It's nothing,' said Morven, 'I can handle it. Let me go after her and I'll sort it out.'

'Certainly not. I want to know exactly what's been going on. I know those Higginses. If she's the girl I think she is, I was at school with her father, and he was bad news from start to finish. So just get in there, sit down and explain to me and your Aunt Linda exactly what you've been up to!'

Linda appeared at the living room door. 'Trouble?' she enquired.

Morven gazed at her two Aunts with clouded eyes. Why did everything have to turn bad, just when it was all going so well? And how was she going to get Angela Higgins, best friend of Charlene MacTell, off her back?

CHAPTER FIFTEEN

The next morning, as Mairi was tidying up after breakfast and before going up to the big house, she announced to her mother, 'I'm going to learn to read and write.'

'Don't forget to close the gate as you go up the hill,' said Jess. 'And take that empty basket back to Lady Janet.'

'Yes, Mother, I will,' said Mairi, 'and while I'm at it, I'll ask her about learning to read and write.'

Jess paused. 'Did I hear you right?'

'Yes, I suppose you did,' replied Mairi.

'*What* did you say you were going to ask Lady Janet about?' Jess's voice was growing sharp.

This was it; Mairi had known her mother wouldn't approve of her plan. 'It'll come in very handy,' she insisted.

'Reading and writing? *Reading and writing?* Handy?'

'Yes, that's right.'

'You're getting ideas way beyond your station, my girl,' said Jess heatedly. 'What do you think the likes of us needs to read and write for? Good grief, even some of the people at the big house can't read and write. It's not for the likes of us. Don't you dare ask Lady Janet about such a thing! You'll make us a laughing stock!'

Mairi said nothing, but hung up the cloth she'd been using for the dishes, and hoisted the twins on her back. 'Don't forget the basket!' called her mother. And as Mairi disappeared up the hill, Jess wiped her hands on her apron and thought, For goodness' sake. Whatever next.'

'LADY JANET,' SAID MAIRI LATER THAT MORNING, AS SHE handed over a freshly pressed batch of clean linen. 'I want to learn to read and write.'

Lady Janet raised her eyebrows. 'Really? What for?'

'I just think it would be a good thing to do. Then I could write letters to people...'

'People?' smiled Lady Janet. 'Well, I can't help you, I'm afraid. I'm not very good at it myself, although Sir Peter keeps telling me I should try to master it.'

'It just seems kind of amazing, the way they fit all those letters together to make sense,' said Mairi.

'You're right,' said Lady Janet, 'but I still can't figure it out. Well, to be fair, I haven't perhaps tried hard enough. I suppose the children may have to learn.'

'If I learned, I could teach them!'

Lady Janet stared at her, open-mouthed. Mairi reddened, finished the job she was doing and folded away her work. 'Will that be all for now, Lady Janet?' she asked, and when Lady Janet nodded, she replied, 'Well I'll get back to the laundry.' When she came out of Lady Janet's chambers, she thought she might go and see Sir Peter. But this would be rather a bold move, and she felt shy about it. She stood in front of his door with her fist raised for a couple of minutes, trying to find the courage to knock; but when one of the maids came up the stairs with a stack of firewood, Mairi lost her nerve and ran off in another direction.

It was nearly time to set the table for luncheon, but she wanted to know straightaway whether there was any prospect of support for her plan. She screwed up her courage and, making sure nobody was watching, she ran back upstairs and quickly knocked on the door of Sir Peter's chambers. Her heart beating wildly, she heard his voice call, 'Come in' – and there was nothing else for it but to turn the handle and walk through the door. He looked up in surprise. 'Can I help you?' he said, 'is something wrong?'

'Excuse me sir, I just wanted to ask you sir,' she bobbed a curtsy, 'I'm sorry to disturb you but...'

'Come on, spit it out,' said Sir Peter, 'I haven't got all day.'

'Sir, can I learn to read and write?' There! that was it out.

'What?'

'If you please sir, I would like to learn how to read and write, so that I can be of better service in your household.' She had thought about this strategy on her way up the hill that morning – surely it would be a help to Sir Peter if he had a literate maid on the staff?

Sir Peter looked astonished. 'Don't be ridiculous, child!' he said. 'Has somebody put you up to this? Really, it's not your place to ask such a thing! Out of the question! Now leave me!' And he turned back to his desk, where he was sorting out a collection of gunpowder cartridges for a forthcoming shoot. Mairi knew when she had gone far enough, and immediately curtsied and left, running back down the stairs, her cheeks burning. She hoped that Sir Peter wouldn't tell her mother about her request – then she would certainly be in trouble. She wondered what Jean-Luc would say if she could discuss it with him. It was hard to imagine – she had to admit that, although she was ready to spend the rest of her life with him, she hardly knew Jean-Luc at all. She imagined he would be somewhat dismissive of the need to learn to read and write, as he was such a steady, sensible, skilled young man, comfortable with his lot in life. But then, it was a skill he had himself mastered, so he obviously saw the point of it. And, she imagined, wouldn't it be wonderful to see the smile on his face on the day when he received a letter from her very own hand? She decided to have a word with Brother Joseph.

The monks had just finished noonday prayers, and she caught Joseph as he was heading to the stables. 'Brother Joseph,' she said, 'may I have a word?' Brother Joseph gazed at her sternly and raised one eyebrow. Mairi took a deep breath. 'I would like to learn to read and write,' she said, 'as I believe it would help me give better service to our masters.' Joseph stared at her in astonishment. She was the first person ever, since his arrival in Scotland, to express such a desire. He'd almost begun to believe his was a lost cause. Someone at last who wanted to read and write?

A servant, however...

A girl.

'I think you'll find, young lady, that reading and writing are not required by women of your class,' and then he added, 'or indeed by women of any class.' And he turned on his heel and walked away.

Mairi was momentarily crushed, then angry. How dare he treat her like shit on his shoe? She turned slow, sad steps towards the kitchen.

How disappointing. Especially as Brother Joseph would probably have to be the one to teach her. It wasn't as if she needed his full attention; she had imagined that she might sit at the back of the class while he was teaching somebody else. But obviously he did not think it was appropriate. Was he right? She wondered for a moment. Why would women need to read and write? Her mother had got by throughout her life without this ability. As had she and her sisters. And then she thought about the letters she wanted to write to Jean-Luc: to find out when he was coming back to her, to find out when she could rely on him helping her bring up his babies. Of course, women needed to learn to read and write! But how?

She remembered her vision of the night before, watching that young girl of the future drawing a picture and writing things alongside it. Why not, indeed?

She went to collect Archie and Fiona from the kitchen where they sat on a mat watching Jean the cook make pastry. On her way back, they bumped into Rodriguez and Anselm, heading for the orchard. Anselm looked at her kindly, and queried, 'How are you today Mairi? You look as if you have the weight of the world on your shoulders. Still planning your pilgrimage?'

Mairi liked Anselm. He was always willing to listen to her. 'I was just asking Brother Joseph about learning to read and write,' she whispered, looking over her shoulder, 'but he didn't seem to think it was a good idea.' Rodriguez looked up. 'Well, if he wants this book written about looking after the orchards, I'm going to need some help.' And he stalked on, obviously cross.

'He's feeling overburdened,' explained Anselm, 'but he's right; he could do with a bit of help.' And he paused. 'I could show you the basics, if you like,' he offered, 'and you can see whether you've got an eye for it. Some people find reading and writing very difficult, but others take to it quite easily. You might find you're one of the latter.'

'Brother Anselm!' smiled Mairi. 'Would you really? That would be wonderful!'

'Come to the top shed where the printing press is kept,' he said, 'let's say half an hour before Vespers. You have to work hard, mind, and concentrate when I'm showing you the letters. Otherwise, you'll be wasting my time. But if we have a short session every day this week, I'll tell you whether I think you could go further. Would that suit you?'

Mairi jumped up and down with excitement, 'Thank you so much, Brother,' she exclaimed, 'I'll see you later! I promise I'll work hard at it!'

For six nights that week, Mairi carried her babies up to the printing press shed and sat opposite Anselm while he explained to her the rudiments of reading and writing. She would have gone on the seventh night too, but Anselm insisted that it was a day of rest. First, he had laid out the little metal letters before her and introduced different shapes as making different sounds. Then he had produced a slate with some chalk and got her to copy out the letters and say the sounds out loud. Soon they were putting different letters together to make words, and Mairi proved to be a quick learner. She was extremely excited at her new skill and couldn't wait to get started again.

'You must keep practising the shapes of the letters,' insisted Anselm. 'Unless you can do them neatly, nobody will be able to read your writing, and that would be pointless. Try writing with a stick in the sand, just to keep practising.' And then he would give her a little test, showing her words on a slate, which he wrote for her to tell him what they were. Soon, she was getting them right every single time. 'I think you need to progress to more formal lessons,' said Anselm. 'I'll have a word with Brother Joseph.'

'Oh no!' said Mairi, 'I'm sure he won't approve!'

'Well, you've proved yourself capable,' said Anselm. 'I'll just see what he says.'

Meantime, Sir Peter had mentioned to Lady Janet that young Mairi had had the effrontery to disturb him in his study – to ask about reading and writing lessons, no less! 'I don't know what has come over her,' said Sir Peter. 'She seems very forward!'

Lady Janet concentrated on her sewing. 'Well, you know,' she said, 'maybe it wouldn't be such a bad idea, as somebody will have to teach the children someday, and I fear I won't be up to the job.'

'The children!' said Sir Peter, 'But there's plenty of time for that!'

'I'm not so sure,' said Lady Janet. 'Patrick is already nearly ten. Sometimes children learn things faster than adults. I'm sorry to say that reading and writing have eluded me. I just can't get the hang of it. Maybe,' she suggested, 'Brother Joseph could teach them?'

As she had expected, her husband dismissed this suggestion immediately. 'Brother Joseph is far too busy for teaching children,' he said. 'What are you saying, that Jess's daughter could learn a little of the alphabet and pass it on to the children?'

'Well, she's a clever girl,' said Lady Janet. 'And Jess has her hands full, keeping her family going after Hugh's death.'

'Some of the neighbours may want to learn to read and write,' said Sir Peter. 'I'll have a word with Joseph. As for the young girl, well I don't see how that could work.' And Lady Janet left it at that; she knew how far to push things.

BROTHER JOSEPH WANTED TO PRESS ON WITH THE ORCHARD book, or more to the point, to get more people reading and writing, so they could read the Bible. However, the time was not yet right for that – Catholics across the country were minded to leave that to the priesthood. In the meantime, it could only help if it showed the printing press to be a valuable instrument in furthering welfare across the land, and the orchard book project was ideal. He discussed it with Sir Peter, pointing out that it would be an excellent thing if some of the local gentry improved their literacy skills, to take advantage of the orchard book once it was written. Sir Peter was very keen on the orchard book; he loved to innovate and was very proud of the improvement of his estate under the stewardship of the monks – especially the innovation of the orchard. Having a book written on his own estate appealed enormously to his pride.

'Is Brother Rodriguez getting on with the writing then?' he asked Joseph.

'Very slowly,' said Joseph. 'It's a question of lining up all those tiny letters for the press. Rodriguez can write the book, but he's not very adept on the printing press.'

'Is it a job for someone with nimble fingers?' asked Sir Peter.

'Yes that would help,' said Joseph. 'But it also needs to be somebody who can read and write.'

'Brother Anselm?'

'Brother Anselm's eyesight isn't so good,' said Joseph, 'and his fingers are somewhat clumsy.' It had been a nightmare trying to get Anselm to use the printing press: so many letters lost, so much time spent scrabbling around on the floor trying to find them again! Brother Joseph wasn't letting Anselm anywhere near the printing press, ever again, if he could help it.

'No point in everybody learning to read and write if there's nothing for them to read,' said Sir Peter.

'Well, there's always the Bible,' said Joseph.

'Yes, yes, of course,' said Sir Peter, 'but we do need this orchard book you know. See what Anselm says.'

Brother Anselm had a straightforward solution for Brother Joseph – even if it wasn't exactly to Joseph's liking. 'She's very nimble, she's a quick learner, and I'm sure she would get the job done far quicker than any of us here,' said Brother Anselm. 'And I happen to know that she has the rudiments of reading and writing, and could probably go on to learn quickly, given the opportunity.'

'Well Brother, I think you're wrong there,' said Joseph, 'I spoke to her just last week, and she was begging me to learn to read and write – so obviously this is not a skill she possesses.'

'Things have moved on,' said Brother Anselm, and he explained the evening sessions he had been spending with Mairi.

Brother Joseph brooded for the rest of the evening and the whole of the next day, considering the benefits and disadvantages of such an arrangement. Finally, he went to Sir Peter and put a proposal to him, 'I will run a series of lessons for the local landowners – and in so doing, I will teach the girl to read and write. So long as she isn't a nuisance and picks things up quickly enough. Once she's a little further on, she will be able to help Rodriguez lay out the blocks for the orchard book.'

Lady Janet, when she heard of this proposal, immediately supported it. 'Then, after she has made some progress, she should take up a tutor role with our children. I know you don't see the urgency of it,' she added to her husband, 'but I think the time is coming when our children must learn to read and write, and here is an opportunity for our own household. Anyway,' she said, 'you would be setting a good example for the other landowners round about.'

SIR PETER, NOT WITHOUT SOME MISGIVINGS, SENT OUT A message to the neighbouring landowners to come to a meeting to discuss reading and writing classes, and Lady Janet approached Jess to discuss the possibility of an eventual post as tutor for her eldest daughter. 'A tutor?' gasped Jess. 'Don't you need to read and write to be a tutor?' And she was not best pleased to find that she was the last to know about her daughter's burgeoning new skills. On the other hand, she couldn't help but be proud of her sudden rise in status. 'That'll impress the young Douglas,' she informed Mairi, with satisfaction, after giving her a good telling off for her temerity.

And so, within a month, young Mairi found herself sitting behind a screen at the back of a makeshift classroom in an anteroom in the big house, while six landowner neighbours, including the young Douglas, laboured at the front of the room, trying to understand Joseph's explanations. She was glad to have been given the grounding by Anselm, and gratified to discover that she was much further ahead than the rest of them. The next morning, she would start work with Rodriguez on the printing press blocks, and then before long, she planned to write the letter that had brought all this about – the letter to Jean-Luc in France, asking him when he would return.

CHAPTER SIXTEEN

Jennifer and Kyle stood anxiously waiting at the bus stop the following Monday morning for Morven. Usually, Morven was the first to arrive, waving goodbye to Ruth as her aunt went off to start her day at the surgery. Today however, she was late – and her friends grew anxious about her missing the school bus. At last, with seconds to go as the bus rumbled into sight, Morven appeared around her street corner and came dashing up to the bus stop to greet her friends. They could see at once that something had upset her – her face even paler than usual, and a sharp crease of anxiety running right across her fore-head. 'What's the matter?' asked Jennifer, 'You nearly missed the bus!'

The bus pulled up, and Morven cast anxious glances up the aisle as she climbed on. Would Angela Higgins be on the bus? She couldn't see her as yet, but she wasn't taking any chances. 'It's nothing,' she mumbled to Jennifer and Kyle, 'Quickly, just get a seat.' Jennifer shrugged and sat down beside another girl, leaving a double seat for Morven and Kyle. 'What's the matter?' whispered Kyle, 'You look terrible.'

Morven was craning over her shoulder to see right up to the back of the bus – and yes, sure enough, there was Angela Higgins in the back seat with her other cronies. She appeared to be paying no attention to Morven, who immediately slunk back down into her own seat. She glanced at Kyle and wondered whether she should confide in him. Normally, she didn't expect her friends to understand her difficulties. Kyle, she was sure, wouldn't understand this particular issue. However, Morven realised she needed a friend in the playground and decided to take the risk. 'I'm in trouble,' she whispered to Kyle, and his eyebrows shot up. 'What kind of trouble?'

Where to begin? 'Do you know that girl in the back row? The one with the blonde hair and the black roots? Don't stare!' Kyle was trying to see the girl that Morven was indicating, and he took a quick glance then huddled down into his own seat again. 'What? You mean Angela Higgins?' he muttered. 'I'd steer clear of her if I were you.'

'Why, what do you know about her?'

'She's vicious. Ask the Walburton twins. You haven't annoyed her, have you?'

'Not yet,' said Morven, 'but I'm going to have to. Listen Kyle,' she added, 'please don't tell anybody else about this, will you promise?' Kyle glanced across the aisle at Jennifer. 'Okay, you can tell Jennifer, I'll tell her myself, but nobody else okay? Promise?'

Kyle nodded.

'I did something stupid,' said Morven. She felt herself growing all red and hot as she confessed to him what she had been up to. 'Okay, I know it was stupid, but I wanted to help Aunt Ruth out, so I started doing a bit of...' she hesitated, 'I got hold of some Easter eggs to sell in the playground,' she said, and catching Kyle's eye, added, 'Okay I stole them from the shops around the school. I was shoplifting.' And she shrunk into her seat in embarrassment at his incredulous gasp. 'Anyway, it was just little things, small eggs, and bars of chocolate and so on, but do you know Charlene MacTell?' Kyle nodded. 'Yeah, that's right, Angela Higgins's best friend. Well, Charlene MacTell offered me a fiver if I could get her one of the big Easter eggs out of that fancy chocolate shop in the High Street.'

'What, Watson's?'

'Yeah, Watson's. So, I got her one, only I asked for six pounds fifty, and she gave me the money. But now Angela Higgins wants one.' Kyle looked concerned. 'Oh boy, you're in trouble if you're getting involved with the Higginses,' he said.

'It's not just that,' said Morven, 'she came to our door on Saturday night when my Auntie Linda was visiting, and in front of Aunt Ruth, she told me she wants one of those eggs too. So now Aunt Ruth knows I've been shoplifting, and so does Auntie Linda, and...' Tears were welling up in Morven's eyes at the humiliation of it all. Kyle's eyes were wide. 'So, what are you going to do?'

'I don't know. What do you think Angela Higgins will do to me when I tell her I'm not getting her an egg?'

'Oh my God, she'll kill you!'

Morven gulped, 'That's what I thought.'

'Tell your guidance teacher!' said Kyle.

'I can't do that; it'd make it worse. Help, Angela Higgins

and Charlene MacTell between them? They'll turn me into dog meat!'

'Maybe the police will get involved,' pointed out Kyle. 'Sometimes the school brings the police in. I heard that about somebody in my cousin's class.'

Morven groaned. She'd had enough dealings recently with the police, the children's panel, identity parades, and all that sort of thing. It made her want to just run away. 'And then there's your social worker,' said Kyle. 'Will she not want to get involved?'

Morven groaned again. Even worse. Kyle's imagination was running ahead of him now. 'Maybe they'll take you away from your Aunt's,' he suggested – and when he saw the expression on Morven's face said immediately, 'I'm sorry Morven, that would never happen, I was being stupid.'

'Well, I'll have to figure something out,' said Morven, 'but I just can't think how to go about it.' The bus was pulling into the school playground. 'Quick,' said Morven, 'let's get out before she does.' And they nimbly got to the front of the queue and disembarked fast while Angela Higgins was still stealing somebody's baseball cap in the back seat. Jennifer caught them up. 'What's going on?' she demanded, and in quick whispers, Morven and Kyle told her about the predicament. 'Oh Morven,' said Jennifer, genuinely horrified. 'Shoplifting! Whatever made you do that?'

'It was just...' said Morven miserably, 'I know, I know, it was a stupid idea. One of my many extremely stupid ideas. The stupidest yet, probably.'

'Anyway,' said Kyle, 'what are *we* going to do about it?' And Morven could have kissed him.

'You've got to tell your guidance teacher,' said Jennifer.

'I'm not doing that,' said Morven, 'they'll get the police, and the police will get my social worker, and then the children's panel will take me away from Aunt Ruth.'

'I didn't mean that!' said Kyle

'Yeah but still, what if she does?' Morven had experienced enough disasters in her life to know that she was skating on thin ice. 'Anyway', she said, lifting her chin, 'I'm not afraid of Angela Higgins!'

Jennifer and Kyle looked at her in disbelief. 'Not *really* afraid. What can she possibly do to me?' said Morven. 'I'm just going to tell Angela that she'll have to get her own egg, and that'll be an end to it.'

The school bell was ringing. Everyone from the Flegg bus had got off and was straggling in towards the school entrance, including Angela Higgins, who was at the very back. 'Just watch me!' said Morven, and she ran over to where Angela's crowd were holding back for a last puff at a cigarette before going into class. Morven stuck out her chin and announced, 'Hey Angela, you'll have to get your own egg!' And then she ran off.

Jennifer and Kyle were aghast. They followed Morven into the register class queues and bunched themselves up around her protectively, thinking to themselves that this would never end well for any of them. They had all taken safe refuge inside their respective register classes before Angela Higgins had a chance to get back to them; but as the next bell rang and Morven filed out of the class, a small child pressed a note into her hand and ran away. Her mouth dry, Morven unfolded the note. It said, 'Back bike shed 1 PM. You're for it.' Her mouth went dry. There was no escaping this.

CHAPTER SEVENTEEN

Tingling with excitement, Joseph surveyed his class. This is what he had wanted for so long! It was a small beginning, but with this little group of six youngsters learning to read and write, the skills would spread, and soon it would be commonplace and, indeed, desirable for the gentry to require their families to learn the new skills. No longer would it be just the monks and the nobility – and not even the majority of them – who possessed these special, powerful skills. To read and write was to engage fully in the world and make it a better place. His imagination roved wide. Families sitting quietly around the table after supper, reading Psalm 139 together –

Lord, you have searched me, and you know me...

If I rise on the wings of the dawn, if I settle on the far side of the sea,

Even there your hand will guide me, your right hand will hold me fast...

Unavoidably, he reflected, as he surveyed his pupils,

there would be certain challenges in teaching this particular gathering. In the past he had only taught monks, who were keen to learn to read Latin – to read the Bible with their own eyes. It was, as they all knew, an amazing privilege. Whereas today's gathering, seated in two rows in front of him, had much less obvious insight. You couldn't really count the girl, out of sight at the back of the class. That was his condition for allowing her to be present – she was to sit quietly and say nothing, and hopefully everybody would forget she was there. The others, however, were as yet unknown to him as learners. There was the young Douglas and his older brother from the next estate; there was Sir Peter and Lady Janet's oldest son, Patrick, aged only 10, and probably too young to be here at all; there was Sir Peter himself on this occasion, although Joseph was fairly certain that his esteemed patron would soon find other more urgent things to do rather than attend the class; there was Murray of Ninebells estate; and there was the factor. In front of the factor, the monk felt a certain pressure, which made him intensely uncomfortable. Somehow, he doubted whether the factor would appreciate the joy of the letters for their own sake. No doubt he would want to turn it into some kind of sordid moneymaking venture. However, Sir Peter had warned him that it would not be politic to make an enemy of the factor, whose financial support for the orchard book project would be invaluable.

Joseph started his lesson with a lecture about the transition of writing from Latin to English – this being a new and exciting discipline for him, and a passion which he felt sure the assembled gathering would share. To his annoyance, however, his pupils seemed disinterested in this. 'Latin?' said

Sir Peter, 'I think we can skip this bit, can't we?' Seeing Joseph's face, he added, 'As you wish of course.'

The other pupils sat quietly, watching to see how Joseph would respond to Sir Peter's comments, and when Joseph hesitated, the factor stepped in calmly and said, 'Quite so, Sir Peter, let's just get on with learning the English version.'

His face burning, Joseph skipped a few stages in his plan and started introducing some letters of the alphabet, describing the sounds which each letter made, and explaining how the sounds would join up to make words. Young Patrick was playing with a spider at the corner of his desk, paying no attention whatsoever. How could Joseph reprimand him in front of his father? He decided to ignore the child and carry on. The others were looking variously blank, bored and puzzled; when he strolled up to the back of the class and peeked behind the screen, it seemed that only Mairi appeared engaged. This was not what he had had in mind.

'Take your chalk,' he ordered the group. 'Now write on your slates exactly as I am showing you...' And for the next twenty minutes, there was a certain concentrated effort as the class members tried to master the shapes Joseph was explaining to them. 'Very well,' said Joseph. 'That's enough. Come back at the same time next week and we will try some more letters.' And he dismissed the class.

BACK IN THE PRESENT, MORVEN'S MORNING DRAGGED PAST. Caught up in a torment of indecision, she blocked out everything that was taking place around her. The normal school day straggled on in an ordered rhythm of bells ringing and pupils emerging from and entering classrooms, teachers teaching. Jennifer, however, even after thinking it through, couldn't get away from the belief that the guidance teacher's role was key in this situation. She wasn't sure whether Mr Taylor would be the most sympathetic – Morven was often late back in the afternoons and he'd had lots of words with her about it. Jennifer's own guidance teacher was Mrs Morrison, Morven's art teacher, and Jennifer thought how much better it would be for Morven if she could enlist Mrs Morrison's support instead. She knew that Morven trusted Mrs Morrison, and that Mrs Morrison believed in Morven's artistic abilities. She figured out a way to bend the rules.

'Mrs Morrison,' said Jennifer as her register class was filing out, 'can I have a word, please?'

'Of course, Jennifer, if it's a quick one, what is it?' Mrs Morrison was already prising the lids off tins of paint for her first class that morning.

'It's just that one of my friends is going to be involved in a fight in the playground at lunchtime, and I wondered what I should do... because you're my guidance teacher and I know you would want me to do the right thing...'

'Well,' said Mrs Morrison, 'do you think this fight will really take place?' When Jennifer nodded vigorously, Mrs Morrison said, 'Sometimes it's best to get the police...' Then to Jennifer she added 'Not you of course, I mean that's what the head teacher will probably do when he finds out. You should tell him right now.'

'The police, Miss? Is that not a bit... a bit...'

'It's community policing, it's what they do nowadays. They're the ones who come and do our talks about drugs and things. Don't worry, it just keeps things above board. We can't be having fights in the playground. Who's the child, anyway?'

'Well,' said Jennifer, 'Angela Higgins is one of them…'

'I thought you said it was one of your friends?'

'It's…' And Jennifer paused and gulped. 'It's Morven McClure, Miss.'

'Morven!' Mrs Morrison immediately started putting the lids back on the paint tins. 'You mean Morven is to fight Angela Higgins?'

Jennifer nodded nervously. 'Well, we can't have that,' said Mrs Morrison briskly, 'Thank you for telling me Jennifer, you can go now.'

Jennifer hesitated. 'But what if…'

'Don't worry, I'll deal with it. And tell Morven from me to keep well away from Angela Higgins! And any other silly fights she gets into!'

Jennifer didn't get a chance to speak to Morven to pass on these developments until the morning interval, and by that time, Morven had stomach cramps and a rash on the backs of her hands. 'You told Mrs Morrison?' she glared at Jennifer. 'How could you do that? She's the only teacher who likes me, I'll never be able to face her again!'

'Well, she said she would sort it out,' said Jennifer, 'and anyway I don't want you being beaten to a pulp! You should be grateful you've got friends who care about you!' Gratitude? Lots of feelings were surging through Morven's skinny body at that moment, but gratitude wasn't one of them. The bell rang, and they all trooped back into class, and for the rest of the morning she quivered and quaked as the one o'clock bell drew nearer.

· · ·

BACK HOME, RUTH WAS READING THE MORNING PAPER. SHE wasn't due to start at the surgery till two, so she had tidied up and was relaxing for an hour before getting ready to go to work. Her phone rang. It was Linda. 'Linda!' she said, 'Is everything okay?'

Linda had texted to say that she'd arrived home safely the night before; however, she told Ruth of what she had been doing since then. 'Those Higginses,' she said, and Ruth was all ears, 'That girl who came to the door the other night – did you tell me her name is Angela?'

'Yes, that's right,' said Ruth.

'Well, I remembered a few things about her grandfather, or maybe he's her Great-Grandfather, I forget how old I am,' said Linda. 'He was in my class at school. The entire family were bad, but he had a brother who wasn't just a brute, he was a coward and a bully, and there was a time when he got into a lot of trouble, and got put away for it. I heard... never mind how, I overheard his brothers talking about it and discovered there were family secrets he would never want people to know about.'

'Really?' said Ruth, 'What secrets?'

'Well it's not that important really,' said Linda, 'all these years later, but I found him on Facebook last night, and I private-messaged him.'

'Who, Angela's Grandad? Or Great-Grandad?'

'Yeah. And I told him to get Angela to lay off Morven or else I would broadcast his brother's actions from sixty years ago. It turns out he's still nervous of some of that information coming out.'

'Oh good grief, Linda, you're getting yourself into trouble, surely.'

'Well we'll see. Anyway, you might get a visit or a call or something from him, so I'm just warning you in advance.'

'Bloody hell, is he violent? Should I call the police?' but Linda was sure it wouldn't come to that.

Just as Ruth was putting the phone down, the doorbell rang. Crossing her fingers she opened it, just a crack, to reveal a woman who was the spitting image of Angela but an adult version, perhaps twice the weight, and with even less charm. Before Ruth even opened her mouth, the woman burst into full flood. 'See you, you and your scabby auntie, he knows fine it was her by the way, does she think his head buttons up the back? My poor Grampa's in a terrible state, and him with a bad heart and all, her and her so-called memory, who the hell does she think she is anyway, raking stuff up from the past? You need to get that Granddaughter of yours sorted out, that's what my advice is Missus, and leave my Grampa out of this, get it?'

Ruth opened her mouth again to speak, but her phone rang. A private number, one she didn't recognise. She turned a shoulder towards the woman on the doorstep, already fearing the worst. 'Hello? Who's this?'

'Hello Ruth, it's Kyle, don't tell Morven I phoned you. Just to see if you can do something about it, Angela Higgins has challenged Morven to a fight in the playground at lunchtime.'

'What?' said Ruth.

'At one o'clock,' said Kyle, 'could you come and do something about it? She'll get pulverised. Don't tell her I phoned.' And he hung up.

Ruth was angry now. She turned back to Angela's mother. 'I don't know what the hell your Angela is up to, but it seems there's to be a fight in the playground at one o'clock, and believe me if my Aunt Linda knows anything that will protect Morven – and incidentally, she's not my Granddaughter, she's my great-niece as you probably well know – then we will not hesitate to use it. So, you'd better get your arse into gear and...'

'One o'clock? A fight in the playground? That'll be right,' said Angela's mother. 'Come on, you and me's going to the school to stop this. Get a move on!' she hissed, as Ruth turned back for jacket and keys. Angela's mother bleeped the locks on her Mercedes, waiting two doors up.

A WIDE ARENA HAD BEEN CLEARED IN THE SCHOOL playground. The entire first and second-year classes stood in a ragged circle, baying for a fight. At one edge of the circle, Morven stood shaking but defiant, with Jennifer on one side of her and Kyle on the other, both urging her to bow out. 'It's not too late!' said Jennifer.

'Come on!' added Kyle, 'just walk away! There's nothing she can do!'

'Nothing she can do? You better believe it.' She took one wobbly step forward. Angela Higgins stood on the opposite edge of the circle with her arms crossed, feet wide, flanked by her gang. Charlene MacTell was holding her jacket. 'Get her, Angela! Get the bitch sorted!'

As Morven stepped cautiously forward, Angela strode right into the centre of the circle. 'Right, you!' she said, hands on hips, 'Let's see if you're as brave as you were earlier on! Ya wee thief!'

That was it. Morven was furious, and a red rage

descended on her. How dare Angela tell the entire school about her shoplifting. She was affronted, and knew she could never set foot in the school again, so embarrassing was the whole situation.

'Come on then,' jeered Angela

'Come on then – if you dare,' hissed Morven.

The crowd was hushed. Kyle was nearly wetting himself with anxiety, and Jennifer could barely stop herself covering her eyes. And then three things happened.

First, Mrs Morrison broke the edge of the circle and calmly walked into the middle. 'Come with me, Morven,' she said, putting a hand out to Morven's shoulder and positioning herself between the two girls. Over her shoulder she said to Angela, 'Off you go then. The bell will be ringing soon.'

Angela and Morven both stood with their mouths open, not knowing how to respond. Their adrenaline was up, they were ready to tear each other's throats out, and no way were going to be put off by this arty-farty ageing hippie. 'Get out of the way, you old bitch!' grunted Angela.

'Don't you dare speak to her like that!' said Morven, and between them they pushed Mrs Morrison to the side and leaned in to each other, fists raised. Then from another corner of the circle came the second disturbance. It was two police officers, a man and a woman, accompanied by the head teacher. 'OK then girls, let's get you out of here and back inside. Your office, Sir?' One of the police officers addressed the head teacher, who nodded. Once again, the two girls ignored them, more determined than ever to get stuck into each other.

However, just as the first push came, so quickly returned

that nobody could remember who pushed first, another voice came floating through across the playground, as two women came striding through the circle. 'Angela Higgins!' came a rasping call, 'Get out of there and stop your nonsense!' Angela already had a fistful of Morven's hair and her mouth dropped open in amazement, 'What?!'

'She's no worth it!' Angela's mother informed her bemused daughter, jerking a thumb at Morven. 'Come on. Leave her to her own wee games. She's no worth your attention. Don't let her get you into any more bother. Come on, Pet.' And she went to steer Angela away from the centre of the circle; Angela still holding tight to Morven's hair, Morven with Angela's jumper grabbed tight in her own fist. One of the police officers stepped in and addressed the adult in the fracas. 'Just a moment, Madam, who are you?'

'Fuck off,' said Mrs Higgins.

'Okay, come with Angela and we'll ask some questions inside,' And he prised Morven's hair out of Angela's hand, and Angela's jumper out of Morven's, steering the Higginses into the school. His partner turned to Morven and Ruth and said, 'And you two had better come with me.' And they all went inside, Morven now shaking all over. The crowd dispersed, muttering. What was all that about, anyway? The bell rang, and the excitement was over. For the moment.

CHAPTER EIGHTEEN

Mairi attempted to slip away quietly at the end of the lesson but was apprehended by the young Douglas. 'Madam!' said Richmond, bowing to her, 'This is an unexpected pleasure!'

'Please stop that,' she said, horrified, 'this is so embarrassing!' as she looked over her shoulder to see if anybody was watching a young nobleman bowing to her, a mere servant.

'Were you in the class?' he asked, 'I expect you had to supervise the child?'

'I especially asked Sir Peter,' she said, 'if I could attend the lessons. I am keen to learn to read and write. But naturally I had to be out of sight.' Even as she said the words, they sounded ridiculous to her, but Douglas took them at face value.

'Well actually,' he said, 'I think you'll find it's rather demanding. Not the sort of thing women generally take to.'

'Did you enjoy the lesson then?' asked Mairi, thinking to herself, 'I'll show him.'

'I enjoy the opportunity to see you, my lady,' replied Richmond, laying his hand on hers. She snatched it away. 'Come now,' he said, 'let me be bold. You and I have a lot of talking to do.' She bobbed a curtsey, 'Perhaps, sir, but not right now; I have my duties to return to.'

He removed his hat and bowed low, 'Till next week then, my dear.' And he strode off.

Joseph had observed this exchange and found it very puzzling. He sought out Sir Peter in his study. 'Young Douglas's wedding,' he broached the subject, 'in three weeks' time, is that correct?'

'That's correct,' replied Sir Peter, 'at Brokenshaw, the home of his cousin and betrothed. You've met his father already, haven't you, at our gatherings here? He is a staunch supporter of the Queen.'

'Are you aware that he is making advances to your servant, the late steward's daughter?'

'Oh well,' said Sir Peter, 'it's no secret that the marriage to his cousin is not a love match. I expect he has taken a shine, given our young servant's comeliness. And in her situation, she can't hope for too much, can she?'

'In her situation? And what situation is that? Unless you are referring to her lowly status as a servant?'

'Well yes that, but also with the babies Joseph, you must have noticed.'

'She has babies? Of her own? I presumed they belonged to some other member of her family.'

'At the plum harvest – were you not aware? My Lady Janet assisted her in her birthing.'

'At the plum harvest! But I believe she's single?'

'That's correct.'

'And who is the father?'

Sir Peter looked at Brother Joseph in astonishment. 'Surely you are aware? Your servant, Jean-Luc, now in France...'

'Jean-Luc? Never!' Joseph shook his head in disbelief. 'This will never do! Yes, I see, she might as well set her cap at any misguided youngster who comes paying her compliments, but I will not have her in my class! And you sought to put her in charge of your children's learning! Sir, forgive me, but I am horrified at the risks you take! You really want a fallen woman to have a place in the upbringing of your own children? This will never do,' he repeated, 'never! As for Jean-Luc,' he added, 'she must have led him astray. Not that I condone his actions.'

Sir Peter was taken aback. What was he going to tell Lady Janet, after she had been so pleased to set this plan in motion? And really, could he allow Joseph to overrule his own judgements? 'Let us not be hasty,' he addressed Joseph, his tone taking on a steely edge. 'We can discuss this another time. And now I must return to my study, having spent the afternoon away from other priorities!' And he turned on his heel and marched off.

Left alone, Joseph shook his head in bewilderment and frustration. To think that Jean-Luc, his trusted servant, had treated his employer so casually, deserting a girl with child and rushing back to France! It was outrageous! He decided he must write to him at once and returned to his library to do so.

· · ·

THREE WEEKS LATER, JEAN-LUC RECEIVED THE LETTER AT HIS family's home in France. This he read in astonishment; although it took three attempts at Joseph's complicated prose style for Jean-Luc to be sure about the meaning. Such strong words! He decided he had better tell his parents about Mairi – although it would be easier if they didn't know the minor detail of the children. And that was another surprise to Jean-Luc – he had known there was a child, and that it was his – but twins? He beamed; double the delight! If he wrote a letter to his beloved, would she find someone trustworthy to read it out to her? This could be tricky. However, his choices were limited. He decided to take the risk. He had acquired some parchment and a quill and some ink and drew these items towards him as he leaned across the bureau in his mother's kitchen after they had all gone to bed.

'*My dear Mairi,*' he wrote, '*My father and mother will welcome you warmly to our home. And also, our children, now that Brother Joseph has told me about them. I delight in them. Please come at once. My address is at the top of this letter. I am sending money for you to pay the ferryman. Cause someone honest to write to me advising when you are due in Calais, and I will come and meet you. My beautiful Mairi de la Strath, I await your arrival with great pleasure. Your fond servant, Jean-Luc.*

ANOTHER THREE WEEKS PASSED: ARCHIE AND FIONA GAVE UP on breastmilk and vigorously imbibed their share of barley bread steeped in warm cows' milk. Mairi worked extra hard to care for her own babes, and to work with Rodriguez on the printing plates, and to set up a system for Lady Janet's children printing plates, while continuing with her normal duties. Meantime she continued to take her place behind the screen at the back of the class every week, to Joseph's annoyance, while he waited for Sir Peter's judgement on the matter. There was a sense of confusion in the air, and although Mairi loved her letters, and the beginnings of an understanding of the hitherto meaningless text, she could feel the tension.

She could see full well that Brother Joseph didn't want to teach her. And yet her only salvation, she believed, would be in learning to read and write. The young Douglas had now wed, as she learned from Lady Janet's lady-in-waiting, who had attended the ceremony along with Lady Janet and Sir Peter and the children. Richmond turned up each week at class, and it was obvious even to Mairi that he had no interest in learning to read and write, but took every opportunity to draw her away afterwards. She didn't know which way to turn. Should she encourage him? Soon enough one of the pigs would have to be slaughtered, and her mother would be looking for a replacement. But it was hardly dignified, she felt, to accept gifts from a young man so recently wed to another. Her mother seemed to believe that this was her only hope of making good in life; but Mairi just couldn't see it that way. Nevertheless, young Richmond was very engaging in his determination to woo her, and she couldn't help laughing and smiling with him while at the same time backing off. How long would he put up with this, she wondered? There were some signs of his growing impatience – like this very morning, when he had reached out a hand and grabbed her breast, squeezing hard. She still wore the shock of it.

And amid all this confusion, came a letter – and this

time, delivered straight to her instead of to Sir Peter. She opened it with trembling hands. There was only one person she could expect to receive a letter from, and sure enough, there was his signature at the bottom of the scroll. She read the words as fast as she could, spelling and deciphering as she went. Thank goodness for her lessons with Anselm, which had given her a far better start than that received by the others in her class. She knew for a fact that none of them would have been able to read Jean-Luc's letter, and that feeling gave her a sense of safety.

So! She put the letter down on her lap. Tears of joy gave way to vexation. 'He expects me to drop everything and go running to him in France! And him only just aware of the responsibility of two small children! What a nerve! How dare he?' And she strode into the kitchen, picked her children up briskly and went slamming down the path to her mother's cottage.

Having settled the twins for the night, she undressed herself and hung up her gown for the next day. In her night-gown, she wrapped her shawl around her shoulders and lit her candle, then sat down to do a little studying before bedtime. She had a little pouch of metal letters from the printing press, and had devised a little game for herself in which she counted out 20 letters at a time, and made as many words as she could from the random selection. She saw that she could criss-cross them to get double use from certain letters, and it was fascinating to her to discover that she could move the letters around to get different combinations.

Tonight, she looked to her letters for inspiration. What with young Douglas's obvious impatience in the morning, followed by the unexpected – though longed-for – letter from Jean-Luc, she felt very discomposed. How on earth should she order her life? She could perhaps settle down as the young Douglas's mistress...but would that really be satisfying? It would probably keep the wolf from her door, and also from her mother's... but surely, she was worth more than that? And what if he tired of her? Where would she, and her babies, stand then? Or she could go to France with Archie and Fiona; and now, at last, she realised how little she knew of Jean-Luc. Not only did she recognise that she might not get on with his parents, what if she didn't get on with him either? Why should he expect her to give everything up over here – to say goodbye to her mother and sisters and brothers, and this new job which surely counted for something – just for his convenience? He ought to take his responsibilities more seriously, she decided. He ought to come over here and get to know the babies – and in fact, to get to know her too. Only then would she be able to decide whether she wanted to return to France with him. Or to make her life with him here, which she recognised as another possibility, and a far happier one. How could she make this happen?

She scattered the letters on the table in front of her and shifted them around a bit. It was exciting for her to discover how many words she now knew and could spell correctly. She fingered among them, picking out the vowels and consonants, and started laying words out in front of her: SWORD she picked out, remembering the silent W after the S. Then, BREAD, coming down from above so that the two words shared a common D. BABY, top right. The leftover letters caused her some difficulties until she remembered the unusual GUE endings which Anselm had explained to her the other night. So that was it, coming in from the left and finishing with the E of bread – PLAGUE.

She had a sense that the words which came to her held special meaning; like someone trying to send her messages from another world. How strange, she thought. Bread and baby were obviously close to her heart, and the major priorities in life, so there was no mystery there. SWORD was unusual, although now that the young Douglas was visiting so regularly, she was more than previously aware of the frequency with which men brandished their swords. But PLAGUE? There had been some reports of stragglers coming up the Strath, looking ill and seeking healing in their pilgrimage. Maybe she should pay more attention to those stories.

As always, she finished her session by holding a collection of letters close in her hands for the warmth and vibration, and with eyes closed, opened herself to messages from the future. And as always, there was the young redheaded child she had come to know. This time she was fiercely standing up to an older girl, and it looked as if she were getting the better of her. 'Well done!' praised Mairi, in encouragement. 'We can win, you and I, even though the odds are stacked against us.' The vision faded and she sat back and opened her eyes and returned to the present. Tomorrow she would figure out what to do next. For now, she would just have to sleep on it. She blew out the candle and crawled into bed, hugging the blankets around her. Yes, she would find a way.

CHAPTER NINETEEN

Astrid was back. 'You're not going upstairs this time,' Ruth had warned Morven in advance, 'leaving me to make your excuses for you. You have to face up to her yourself this time.'

They were sitting in the living room, Astrid with her arms folded on the sofa, Morven on the floor, and Ruth in the armchair. 'Okay then, Morven,' said Astrid, 'tell me the whole bit about the shoplifting. After that you can tell me the whole bit about bullying. Then you can tell me what your plans are for the future.' Morven wriggled uncomfortably; this was going to be a nightmare. 'Come on then,' continued Astrid, 'start with the shoplifting.'

'It was just wee things,' said Morven, and seeing her aunt flinch, added, 'I know I shouldn't have done it though.'

'What were you doing with the things you stole?' asked Astrid.

'Selling them,' muttered Morven.

'Say that again?' said Astrid.

'Selling them.' repeated Morven, a little louder.

'To whom?' Morven just looked at her. 'Who were you selling them to?' said Astrid.

'Just people in the playground.'

'What sort of things did they buy from you?'

'Sweeties, chocolate eggs and things.'

'So how many times a week did you go shoplifting for stuff to sell?'

'Once or twice.'

'And what did you do with the money?'

It was Ruth's turn to wriggle in embarrassment. However, she kept quiet for the moment, to allow Morven to tell the story in her own way. She would have to discuss all this with Astrid later on.

'I hid it in Auntie Ruth's purse.'

Astrid looked at Ruth. 'I presume you didn't know about this?'

'Certainly not!' Ruth was affronted at the very idea. Morven chipped in, 'I was just trying to help.'

Ruth was sitting with a red face and rigid shoulders; Morven was pale and tense; Astrid was looking from one to the other in irritation. 'But you knew the kinship money was coming through!' she said to Ruth.

'I think we can discuss the money later, Astrid, just you and I,' said Ruth stiffly. Astrid met her eyes and nodded. Fair enough. 'Okay then Morven,' she said turning back to the girl, 'so where does Angela Higgins come in?'

Haltingly, with the minimum of detail, Morven explained the scenario about Charlene MacTell and Angela Higgins to her social worker. 'So, are these two girls what you might call bullies?' asked Astrid, and Morven nodded. 'But I'm not scared of them,' she said.

'Well maybe you should be,' said Aunt Ruth.

'How did you get them off your back then?' asked Astrid, and Ruth explained her Aunt Linda's surprise intervention with Angela's grandfather. 'Small town politics,' she added, 'Memories go back a long way.'

'Just as well for you then Morven,' said Astrid. 'So – now I've got to write another report for the children's panel, and they will want to know whether this is something they can expect more of in the future. Just when things were settling down,' she added.

'We've had that conversation,' said Ruth. 'I believe Morven when she says there won't be any more shoplifting.' Morven shifted a little closer to her aunt.

'I was considering ending the supervision requirement,' said Astrid, 'but I don't see how I can argue that now. The panel has the police report, and they'll be concerned that your behaviour will deteriorate again.

'Listen to me carefully Morven – and you too Ruth. I know you don't like it when I come along and pester you with these questions. But I've seen too many placements – yes, even though I'm young and you think I have no experience, Ruth – I've seen too many placements break down in adolescence, when situations which seemed perfectly settled suddenly blow up. I absolutely do not want that to happen here, and I'm sure you don't either. Ruth, you've been through all this before with Aileen. Morven – I'm sorry if this sounds brutal, but you really don't want to end up like your mother, do you?' And Morven's eyes grew black and angry. 'Do you?'

repeated Astrid, and Ruth gasped at the social worker's persistence. Morven dropped her head into her hands to hide a sudden tear that sprang to her eyes, and Astrid said, 'I'll take that as a No then. Okay, you can go upstairs while I speak to Ruth. I'll be back next week though.' Morven quickly sprang to her feet and ran upstairs before Astrid changed her mind again, and they heard her bedroom door slam.

Ruth looked at Astrid, 'That was a bit tough, wasn't it?' she said, and Astrid raised an eyebrow. 'Okay then,' said Ruth, 'I know you need to make her understand. But please don't question me about money in front of Morven. You knew very well that finances were tight here, and I don't think you have understood just how difficult that was for me. However, I'm sorry that I allowed Morven to recognise it, because now I see that was why she decided to go shoplifting. Believe me when I tell you how much I regret that.'

Astrid nodded. 'Well now that the carer's allowance is through, are you going to cope financially from now on?'

'I still haven't heard how much it'll cost to have my car fixed, so for the moment we're without a car. Apart from that though, yes we'll be fine.'

'I'm not your enemy,' said Astrid. 'I just don't want to see Morven going off the rails, and I know that would break your heart too. She is lucky to have you as her aunt, and maybe I haven't said that to you before, Ruth. I'm sorry if you feel taken for granted. But yours is the best, and the last, chance she'll get, and that's what's keeping her from going the same way as her mother. I'll do whatever it takes to prevent that from happening, even if it makes you both hate me.'

.   .   .

LINDA PHONED LATER THAT NIGHT TO SEE HOW THE DREADED meeting had gone, and Ruth could tell her that actually it was all right. 'She is a pain in the arse,' she said, 'and I could see her far enough, but she has a tough job to do. And it's true enough, it would be so easy for Morven to go the same way as her mother, and that's what terrifies me too. So, in some kind of funny way, Astrid and I are actually on the same side.'

'How's Morven feeling then?'

'Away to bed looking very sheepish. Very apologetic. And aware that I have to go into the school and try to make it all right with her guidance teacher. She says she hates school, and I don't really know how to help her with that.'

'Are you still coming up to me next weekend?' said Linda, and Ruth agreed that they were indeed. 'We can talk things over then,' said Linda, 'and don't forget, Ruth, you're welcome here at any time, and I'll do whatever I can to help. You're doing all the right things.'

'Well thanks,' said Ruth. 'Sometimes I wonder. Anyway – thanks for phoning – see you on Friday night.'

MORVEN'S GUIDANCE TEACHER WAS OFF SICK THE FOLLOWING day when Ruth called at the school, so on a whim, she asked to speak to Mrs Morrison, who immediately agreed. Mrs Morrison had been Ruth's own art teacher many years before when she was in second year. She didn't expect Mrs Morrison to remember her, but she had strong memories of the teacher. Although she hadn't considered herself good at art, she had liked the relaxed atmosphere in the classroom, and it was one of her better school memories. But Mrs

Morrison surprised her by saying at once, 'So it is you, Ruth! I thought you might be the Aunt that Morven was staying with. I remember you well; and Aileen.'

'Gosh you've had the whole family!'

'Yes well, that's what happens when you grow old,' laughed Mrs Morrison, 'isn't Linda Farrier also related to you somehow?'

'Yes, she's my aunt, my mother's sister,' said Ruth, 'how do you know her?'

'I've seen some of her work,' replied Mrs Morrison, 'it's highly rated. I love it.'

'Really? I'd no idea.'

'She's a great artist,' said Mrs Morrison, 'However let's talk about Morven. You know she's very talented, don't you?'

'Yes I do; she decided a little while ago that she wanted to go to art school, and I was delighted to hear her say it, but really, she struggles in all her other subjects, and I don't know how to advise her.'

'Well you can be an artist without going to art school,' said Mrs Morrison, 'just ask your Aunt Linda. What you want for Morven is for her to be happy. If she can be happy by forcing herself to settle in at school and pass the exams, and go the traditional route to art school, then that's fantastic. But if that doesn't make her happy then she can be an artist, anyway. And if she wants to, she can go back to art school later in life – lots of people have done that.'

'I hadn't thought of that,' said Ruth. 'How do you mean, she could be an artist without going to art school?'

'She just has to keep being creative, following her nose. Don't worry too much about jobs for the moment; something will turn up over the next few years. Is she still with the children's hearing system?'

'Yes, and I don't know if she still will be after this recent episode; we need to wait and see.'

'Oh well – just play it by ear then,' said Mrs Morrison, 'make sure she keeps on drawing, if you can, and if she's still enjoying it, because she has talent. And talent doesn't go anywhere without hard work. And the most important thing – I think it makes her happy.'

'It does, she's very relaxed and focused when she's drawing and painting.'

'I'm always here for her, and for you too Ruth, don't forget that.'

'Thank you so much, Mrs Morrison. I'm so grateful.'

AND SO THAT WEEKEND WHEN THEY WENT TO ARBROATH, THE atmosphere was considerably calmer than it had been for the last week or two. Morven felt sheepish in front of Linda, but Linda soon dispelled that. Ruth repeated to Linda, in front of Morven, what Mrs Morrison said – about Linda being a talented artist herself.

'Really?' said Linda. 'That was very kind!'

'So, what kind of artist are you then?' asked Morven.

'I don't know,' said Linda, 'I don't know if there's a name for it. But I'll show you my work if you're interested.' Absolutely – they both were. And Linda took them on a tour of the back gardens of Arbroath, pointing over hedges and walls at various features which she had designed and put in place, waving at the owners, introducing Ruth and Morven to her various clients. 'I'm a garden designer I suppose, or maybe sculptor, or installer,' she said, 'although some of my stuff is a bit offbeat for some people's taste. And I don't have any qualifications in gardening or garden design. It's just the living world which is so fascinating to me. It's more like sculpture than drawing, really, because it's in three dimensions. But there's a something extra too, something kind of spiritual.'

'Like the labyrinth?' said Morven.

'Yes actually, that's a good example. Like the labyrinth.'

They went home for tea and relaxed in each other's company. The crisis was over. Morven wouldn't do any more shoplifting – the very idea made her wince – and Ruth would stop worrying about the money, and adjust and make the best of what she had. For the moment, there was no car, and that was a loss; however, there was an excellent bus service so all would be well. After Morven had gone to bed, and Linda had poured them both a glass of wine, Ruth broached a new subject with Linda. 'You know that conversation we had about my job?' Aunt Linda nodded. 'I've been looking into it, and you're right. I've been a wimp. The more I think about it, the more I think I should train as a vet nurse, not just do the minimum I need to do to keep my job as Vet Assistant. I would earn far more, but more to the point, I think I'd be a good vet nurse!' And she blushed a little and laughed. 'And I think I'd enjoy learning about it properly. You know, the reasons things get done a certain way, and so on...

'Plus,' she said, 'if I go part-time next year to go back to college for my Highers, I'd have more time to spend with Morven, and that would be really nice. We probably both need that.'

'Can you afford it?' asked Linda.

'I'll sort things out so I can afford it,' said Ruth; 'I've been looking into getting the mortgage extended. And maybe do a bit of dog walking, but I'd charge people for it properly this time. We'll get by. Mince and tatties. Macaroni Cheese! It'll be worth it in a few years' time when I can earn so much more.'

'What made you change your mind?'

'Well, I hate to admit it...'

'What?'

Ruth laughed and threw up her hands in despair. 'Do you know what kind of car Angela Higgins's mother drives?'

'No?'

'A Merc.'

'What, a Merc as in Mercedes?!'

'The very one.'

'Ouch.'

'I know.'

'Well here's to you both,' said Aunt Linda, raising her glass, 'whatever you end up driving – let it be a great journey!'

CHAPTER TWENTY

Mairi checked her letter for the tenth time and wished she had someone who could check it for her. 'Oh well,' she shrugged, 'if it's full of mistakes at least he'll know I'm thinking about him. And his message. And what I've decided.' So, she signed it at the bottom, as Anselm had advised, rolled it up with the address Anselm had found for her, and tucked it into her pillowcase till the next time she would see Beth.

Dear Jean-Luc,

as you see I write with my own hand.

I am happy to hear from you. But do not ask me to come to France. It is too far, and I need to be close to my family. You must come and meet Archie and Fiona and decide whether your home is in Scotland.

I remember you fondly,

Mairi

Mairi did not know how to have her letter delivered to Jean-Luc in France, but had considered that probably her sister Beth, working for Cunningham the Factor near Perth, could find this out and even take her letter to the post somehow. Cunningham was in her reading and writing class, and from her hidden position at the back of the room she had heard him boast once or twice that he was in the habit of sending and receiving letters from all around Scotland and beyond. Even though, as she guessed, he was as slow at his letters as the rest of them. He was such a blow-hard and she did not trust him and would not give him any sign of her personal business. Beth and Peggy were coming to visit the following Sunday; she would speak to Beth then.

Her mother, Jess, was busy all week, excited at the prospect of having all her family around her again. How her life had changed in the last year! Hugh gone, and Beth and Peggy away in service. And Mairi embarked on an unexpected line of work, one which Jess didn't understand at all but might lead to good things. Home life felt so different – and yet she knew it was for the best and was very thankful to have found a means of support for all three of her daughters and her two little grandchildren. The boys, she could manage and in due course it would be more straightforward for them to get jobs, hopefully on the estate. The time may yet come when Sir Peter would need her house for an incoming worker; at least she didn't have all those other children to worry about. Jess felt old before her time. She was only 34 and her life had been tough. But maybe it wasn't over.

She rose early on the Sunday morning to collect fresh nettle tops to brighten the barley. Jean, the Cook at Glenmiglo, had slipped her the remains of a rabbit and a hen which had fed the family during the week; and she was about to boil them up in a tasty stew, to spoon over the savoury barley. There were some apples still in store, and she brought them out to make a sweet pudding. Mairi helped set the table before they all walked down to Ninebells Road to meet the girls. Life had dealt Jess some severe blows, but she was a resilient woman. These days, when her daughters returned home, provided the greatest fun she had ever had in all her life – days to savour, long after the event. She even made the boys wash their faces, to their disgust, and dried them roughly with the end of her sacking apron.

Spring was picking up: there were buds on the trees, and the occasional tiny peep of pink as a little blossom tried to escape. The day was fair but cool, and perfect for the long walk. As always, Beth and Peggy were excited and chattered non-stop all the way back up to the cottage. Before going into the house, they ran round the back to inspect the progress of the piglets, which were growing nicely – no doubt in the autumn, they would sacrifice one of them for the winter larder. Jess was quietly confident that Mairi would provide another to take its place.

Peggy had brought cheese again from the dairy at Ninebells estate, courtesy of Lady Murray. Jess cut off a little sliver so that they could all taste it, and they nodded and approved it very much. 'I made it myself,' said Peggy, and when her mother and sisters looked at her in disbelief, she added, 'well at least I helped.'

'Do you think the cows get better grass up at Ninebells, because of the way the fields catch the sun?' asked Beth, 'And that's why maybe their milk is sweeter and gives us better cheese?'

Mairi found this an interesting question – it was the

same kind of discussion she often heard the monks engaging in.

'Does it make all that much difference,' asked Jess, 'to the grass?'

'Well some of our fields get very boggy until the sun gets at them, don't you think, mother?' said Mairi. 'Sometimes the cows are up to the knees in glaur!'

'His Lordship is always trying to think of ways to make a better profit,' said Peggy. 'That's why he's so pleased at Sir Peter giving the monks a refuge. He says the monks are clever at farming.'

'Aye, so they say,' said Jess. 'Your father would never believe it though. So, what about you, Beth? How are things up at Cunningham's?'

'Fine, mother,' said Beth. 'He is keen on his profits too. You see him every Friday night in his study, counting out all the pennies from the week's work.'

'Doesn't he keep the door closed?' said Jess. 'Sir Peter would never do that in public view.'

'Yes, the door's shut, but I have to take him a little tray at seven o'clock, with a jug of whisky and a plate of scones and butter. That's how I know what he does.'

'Oh my! Whisky, scones and butter? See How the Other Half Lives!' hooted Jess, and they all had a bit of a chuckle at the notion of Cunningham in his nightgown, counting up the pennies.

'He's good at the counting,' said Mairi. 'He comes to the big house every week now for reading and writing lessons, but what he is best at is numbers and weights and measures.'

Jess gave a hollow laugh. 'We'd all be better off if we understood the figures better,' she said. 'It's easy enough to cheat us when we can't count up the money the same way as he does.'

'Well, I've got a little gift for all of you,' announced Mairi. A gift? The girls were delighted. Now that their sister was working in the big house, there was no saying what she might bring home. 'What is it?' they queried.

'Here,' said Mairi, reaching into a package she had brought that morning from the big house. And she extracted a little sheaf of papers and passed out slips to each one of them.

'What's this?' said the boys, prepared for disappointment.

'I know,' said Peggy, holding up her slip of paper to the light, 'I think this is my name, isn't it?'

'That's right!' said Mairi, 'Well done! How did you know?'

'Lord Murray has a list with all the staff's names on it,' said Peggy, 'and one day I asked the housekeeper to show me which one was my name. It's got these three long legs at the end,' she pointed.

'You've all got your own name written here on your slips of paper,' said Mairi, 'and I'm going to teach you all to write your name.'

Oh yes, everyone was enthusiastic about that. Even Jess acknowledged that if ever any of them got married, it would be wonderful to sign their own names on the certificate, rather than scrawl a cross, as she had done. Having been dead against Mairi asking for reading and writing lessons, she had begun to understand the advantages. And so, they spent half an hour with charcoal and paper until they all felt pleased with the results.

'Is it hard, learning to read and write, Mairi?' asked Beth.

'It just takes a bit of concentration and practice. I'm to teach Lady Janet's children.'

'Teach the big house children!'

'Eventually. Lady Janet says she's too busy. And she thinks the children should learn. She's right – you should all learn too.'

Jess changed the subject before the others could respond. 'So, Beth, does your housekeeper still keep up with the blacksmith at Flegg?'

'Yes, I think so,' said Beth., 'Arthur often brings horses and coaches and other jobs back to Mr Cunningham from the Forge, and when he does, his wife is usually with him. Agnes takes her into the pantry and they have a little goblet of wine along with their pikelets!'

'Wine!' said Jess, 'Well I never! You wouldn't catch the servants at Glenmiglo stealing the boss's wine.'

'I don't think Agnes sees it as stealing,' said Beth.

'Well,' said Jess firmly, 'it is stealing, and don't let me ever hear of you doing such a thing.'

'No mother!' said Beth, shocked. 'I never would!'

'And I hope you don't address him as Arthur!'

'I don't address him as anything, he doesn't pay any attention to the rest of us. What else should I call him?' But Jess didn't have an answer to that; 'Mister' was for the gentry, and Arthur was a tradesman – a good one, as she remembered from her late husband's comments.

Mairi asked Beth to help her tidy away the dishes and wash them down at the burn after the meal was over. She took the chance to ask her whether she could get a letter in the post for her. 'A letter?' said Beth, 'From you?' Her eyes were round. 'You can write letters?'

'Yes,' said Mairi, 'what about it?'

'Oh nothing. Who are you writing to?'

'None of your business,' said Mairi. Then she relented – after all, she needed Beth's support. 'Actually, it's a letter for France,' she said.

Beth gasped, 'Really! For Jean-Luc?'

'Shhh!' said Mairi, 'No need to tell everybody! Will you be able to get it posted for me, that's what I want to know? And also, have you any idea how much it costs?'

'Agnes takes letters to a place in Perth for Mr Cunning-ham, and they go off with the coach and horses. I could slip your letter into the pile – I don't think Agnes would notice, because I'm sure she can't read herself. But I've no idea how much it costs. Why don't you just give me your letter anyway, and I'll slip it into the pile, and probably she won't notice any extra charges because there's always lots of letters, anyway?'

Mairi was a little dubious about this. She would rather have paid for it herself, so she would know it had definitely been dispatched. But she didn't know how to go about it, so she agreed and slipped the letter from her apron pocket into Beth's. 'Don't tell mother, mind,' she commented, and Beth nodded back. They both knew there were things that it was safer their mother not knowing.

MAIRI CALCULATED THAT SEVERAL WEEKS WOULD PASS BEFORE she heard back from Jean-Luc. She felt relieved to have opened up a direct line of communication with him – so much better than depending on catching titbits of news third and fourth hand. However, she worried a little that she may have put him off completely. It sounded as if his parents could give him a good living at home so why should he bother coming all the way back to Scotland? He could simply forget her, forget about his responsibilities to the children, and nobody would ever expect him to do otherwise, because probably they didn't even know she and the babies existed. No doubt his parents would rather he found a pretty little French girl to marry.

Meantime, she had plenty to occupy her in progressing her studies in reading and writing, and in the beginnings of discussions about the publication of the orchard book. Mr Cunningham the factor had agreed to put up the money for the book, and Rodriguez was busily putting together his plans for its contents. He had asked Sir Peter to find him some help in assembling the printing blocks, and after some thought, Sir Peter had recommended that Mairi be tasked with this job.

'The maid?' uttered Rodriguez in disbelief. 'You mean the nursemaid? The late steward's girl?'

'Yes, that's right,' said Sir Peter grimly, 'Brother Joseph may not agree with this, but she is by far the best student in the class. And she has the nimble little fingers you need for those blocks. See how you get on with her.'

And so, Rodriguez just had to accept this, and an uneasy working relationship grew up between the monk and the housemaid as he began to recognise her competence.

Young Douglas found it more difficult to steal some time with Mairi after classes as she was always busy. However, he persevered, and became ingenious in his attempts to trap her. Mairi still didn't know how to deal with him. She didn't really want to become somebody's part-time mistress, with no say at all in a relationship. On the other hand, he was charming, and despite his steadily growing boldness, she found him really quite attractive. Her only previous sexual experience had been those two delightful nights with Jean-Luc, which had awakened her to a world she had hitherto known nothing of. She could imagine that with the young Douglas, there would be a great deal more fun of the same kind. And yet... if only Jean-Luc would come back to her! Surely that would be better?

She grew steadily more adept at ducking and avoiding young Douglas's manoeuvres, and sometimes he laughed at this and enjoyed the chase – at other times she could see the beginnings of a temper. Men's temper, she had had enough of with her father. She didn't want to incur the young Douglas's wrath. That would be just too frightening. She wasn't sure how long she could keep him at bay.

And meantime, Jess's cottage became ever more plastered with little slips of parchment and words written on them – words Mairi intended to learn, and which she could practise over and over again – orchard, pears, apples, plums, seeds, bare-root trees, splicing, bushels, hectares... And every night she scattered the little letters and meditated on them, communing with her great great great great granddaughter of many generations hence.

CHAPTER TWENTY-ONE

Kyle had an idea for earning some extra pocket money and wanted Morven to do it along with him. 'I don't want to do it on my own,' he said, 'it's too boring. But it would be okay if we both did it.'

'What do you want extra money for?' asked Morven.

'I'm saving up for a new bike. I want one with off-road capability, and Dad says I have to earn half of it. He'll give me the rest for my birthday and Christmas together.'

'You could get a paper round,' suggested Morven. 'That's what Aunt Ruth said I could do.'

'Yeah, but I don't think they're taking anybody else on just now,' said Kyle. 'People read the news online instead of buying a paper.'

'Well, I could do with earning some extra money too,' said Morven. 'I need to pay the money back to the shops that I stole the sweeties from, and it's taking me ages to save up.'

'How much do you need?'

'Thirty-two quid.'

'Well,' he said, 'we could probably manage that with this idea of mine, and I don't think it would take us all that long to make thirty-two quid – each.'

'So, what's the idea then?' said Morven, interested by now.

'I thought we could wash cars in the car park, at the Open Gardens day.'

'Wash cars... When's that?'

'Couple of weeks away, in June. All we need is a couple of buckets and sponges, and I suppose some car shampoo which my Dad's already got. He says he would donate it to the cause. And there's a tap at the back of the car park, so it would be easy enough.'

'Will there be enough cars?'

'Yeah, there's loads of people come visiting on Open Gardens day. We could charge them a fiver each.'

'A fiver? Never!'

'Okay, so what do you think we could charge?'

'Three? Three pound-fifty? What do you pay if you take your car to the proper car wash?'

'Well there are different programs, you get a basic wash for about four pounds I think, and then you pay extra for polishing and so on. Wheel hubs and all that. My Dad usually goes for the basic and makes me do the wheel hubs.'

'So... why don't we give it a wash and a bit of a polish, and charge four pounds, and maybe some people will just say keep the extra pound so we'll get a fiver anyway?'

'Two-fifty each?'

'Yeah, split it down the middle.'

'Yeah that's what we'll do. Great idea.'

.   .   .

RUTH HAD BEEN VERY FIRM WITH MORVEN ABOUT THE NEED TO pay back the money, and to Morven's enormous embarrassment, had taken her on a tour of the sweetie shops in Glenbuckie where she had stolen the confectionery. In each case, the shopkeepers were bemused but grateful for Aunt Ruth's intervention. They all suffered from shoplifters on a regular basis, and it was a constant drain on their efficiency. Morven had estimated that she had stolen about £40 worth of sweets altogether, and along with Aunt Ruth had committed herself to handing £14 back into each of the three shops, which the shop managers would then put into their charity boxes. Now that she had started, it felt like a project and she was keen to complete it; however, it felt like it would take a while. Twice she had been asked to draw doggy portraits for dogs which she walked with Aunt Ruth. This was satisfying for her, although she wasn't sure Mrs Morrison would approve. It wasn't easy to draw the dogs from life, because they wouldn't sit still long enough, and she always ended up resorting to copying from photographs. However, the results weren't bad, and the owners were quite pleased about it, and on each occasion gave her five pounds for her work. Other than that though, apart from giving up part of her pocket money each week, she couldn't see how she would get the rest of the money together for the shoplifting reparation. So, Kyle's idea was a welcome one.

Kyle's Dad suggested they practise on his car, and it was just as well they did because they discovered that there were several deficits in their performance. 'It's a learning curve,' said Kyle's Dad. 'You need to do it properly or you can't take money off people.' They persevered, and by the time Open Gardens day came along, they were proud to take up position in the car park with their homemade sign offering car washes for four pounds a time.

From noon onwards, the cars came rolling in, and at least half of the garden-viewers were happy to have their car washed while they went off to visit Flegg's hidden gardens. However, there was then a long wait before people came back to collect their cars and pay the money, so Kyle and Morven took turns at nipping over to the church hall for the use of the toilet and to scrounge a bun. The church was in full fundraising mode, selling tickets for the Open Garden events, and with a nice side-line in potted plants. Jennifer's Mum was selling tickets at the door and put together a little package of home baking for them to munch on while they waited in the car park.

By five o'clock, all the customers had collected their cars and driven away, their owners having cheerfully handed over their fivers for Kyle and Morven's work. The pair had enjoyed working together, and knew that they were doing a good job, not leaving any streaks, and buffing the clean cars to a nice shine after washing off the suds. They squatted down, emptying their pockets to count their takings – and were pleased to find that they had sixty pounds to split between them. Thirty quid each! Morven was ecstatic. Only another two pounds, which she would take off her pocket money, and that was the shoplifting reparation project dealt with, and the whole sorry humiliating episode consigned to the past. Tired, soggy, and proud, she and Kyle straggled off home, swinging the buckets behind them.

Ruth firmly approved of Morven's response to the situation. She was due to finish work early on the Monday, so she agreed to meet Morven after school in Kinbuckie and go on a tour of the three shops so they could hand over the money. Afterwards, they got the bus back to Flegg, and picked up a pizza in the Co-op before going home for tea. 'Right,' said Ruth, 'I'm going to write to Astrid now and ask her to call an early review of your hearing. I'm sick of going along to these awful children's panels, and I know you are too. Let's convince them it's no longer necessary, okay?'

'Why don't I write my own letter as well?' Said Morven. 'That usually impresses adults.'

'Okay,' said Ruth, and they sat down and wrote their separate letters. Ruth's letter asked Astrid to put an end to the supervision requirement, because Morven had taken responsibility for her actions by paying back the money she had stolen from the shops and had otherwise settled down well at Ruth's. Morven's letter started, *Dear Astrid,* and continued,

... I don't need anybody else looking at how I'm getting on because Aunt Ruth looks after me really well and I was only under the panel because my Mum couldn't look after me properly, and now I know I will be okay and I will not do any more shoplifting. I have washed lots of cars and given the shops £14 each to pay for the chocolate I stole and they're putting it in their charity tins and I did it with my friend Kyle by washing cars. I am going to be an artist and I have drawn some doggy portraits and if you've got a dog I'll draw yours for free although people usually give me five pounds. My Aunt Ruth is going to study to be a vet nurse instead of just a vet nurse assistant and I will help her. We don't need the children's panel to make us do that, we are happy to do it for ourselves. Please don't make me go back to the children's panel. Yours faithfully, Morven McClure

When Astrid received these letters, she argued a bit that

it was too soon after the previous hearing –the one that was called because of the shoplifting. 'We haven't left enough time,' she pointed out. 'Let's leave it another three months.'

Ruth and Morven had a little grumble to themselves about this. However, now that things had settled a bit, Astrid really didn't visit all that often, so they agreed to wait – not that disagreeing would have made any difference as Ruth pointed out, Astrid would have done it her own way anyway.

This meant that Ruth's own plans had advanced considerably by the time the hearing came along. She had agreed with her boss that she would change her hours from the end of July, taking three weeks' holiday, then dropping to 15 hours a week to enable her to take up part-time study. This would give her a break to spend with Morven, and then she was to start college at the beginning of September in Kinbuckie. There she would study maths and English and a few other subjects, including computer skills, which hopefully would mean that a year later she would get a place on a vet nursing course. Her heart was in her mouth just thinking about it.

And so, September was eventful. Morven had started into second year at school, and then Ruth started at college, also in Kinbuckie. There was a gentle start with introductions and tours of the library, and she discovered she wasn't the oldest in the class – in fact there were three others around her age, all of whom felt much as she did about their past school achievements. However, they were given a written assignment at the beginning of Week Two, and at that point panic and terror set in. She was sure she would fail the assignment, and was certain that she would have to give the course up and go crawling back to Annabel to ask for her old job back.

The children's hearing was scheduled for the last week in September, and Ruth's ordeal lasted for about ten days, while the tutor marked the assignments. It was excruciating; however, her new friends all felt the same way, so they clung to each other and decided to stick with it at least until they got their results.

Morven meantime trundled along without incident at school – not wanting to prejudice her chances of finishing with the children's panel and secretly intensely impressed at her Aunt's courage in taking on the college challenge.

Then, the day before the Hearing, Ruth got her first assignment back with an A pass. Her excitement knew no bounds, although she was sure they had made a mistake, and would surely find her out the next time. Then a helpful tutor spent five minutes with her and helped her see that she really was capable, and could probably achieve her Highers and do vet nurse training. She had never felt so good about herself in all her life. The children's hearing? Bring it on!

The Panel members sat opposite them across a heavy wooden polished table. At the top end, the reporter sat with her files and reports, and made sure everybody understood the legal requirements, and Astrid sat at the bottom. The panel member in the middle introduced everybody and asked Astrid first of all whether she had anything to add to the report she had written.

Astrid had given Ruth and Morven a copy of her report, which recommended that the supervision order be 'terminated'.

'Terminated?' asked Morven, as they sat in the waiting room beforehand, 'I don't like the sound of that.'

'Finished. It just means finished. The supervision order, dumpling, not you!' laughed Ruth.

Astrid replied to the panel chairperson, 'I have nothing to add, thank you. Both Ruth and Morven have worked very hard at settling down together, and I feel they can now get by without any need for supervision.'

'Mrs Farrier, what about you? I see you've just started a college course?'

'That's right,' said Ruth. 'I will acknowledge that it has been quite a challenge at times, for Morven and me to sort things out. But it's much better now than it has ever been, and I'm comfortable that we will manage just fine.'

'And Morven,' continued the panel chairperson, 'tell us how you feel about staying with your Aunt Ruth?'

Morven hated this, having to state the obvious over and over again. However, Ruth had warned her not to be rude, so she just said, 'Yes it's good thank you.'

One of the other panel members chimed in, 'And how are you getting on at school?'

'Fine.'

'How about your art classes? I hear you're very talented,' said the other panel member, and Morven just nodded.

'If you needed help again in the future,' said the chairperson to Aunt Ruth, 'would you feel able to approach the social work department?'

Ruth knew that there was only one correct answer to this; she had to appear as reasonable as she could and therefore accept the prospect of voluntary help if they needed it. But she also knew that in reality, Astrid would be far too busy to offer help on a casual basis. She and Astrid had acknowledged this between them. 'Oh yes,' she said enthusiastically,

'I know that Astrid would always be there for us. I would have no hesitation at all in going to her for help. It's been so useful through the last couple of years.' She glanced at Astrid and wondered whether the social worker would come out with her usual blunt remarks, but Astrid said nothing.

'And you, Morven,' said one of the other panel members, 'would you ask for help if you needed it?'

'Uh huh.'

Finally, the children's panel decided that there was no further need for a supervision requirement to apply in the case of Ruth Farrier and Morven McClure, and the order was terminated. They walked out of the children's panel offices into the shopping mall, leaping for joy. 'Yes!' said Morven, punching the air. 'Yes!' said Ruth, giving Morven a high five. No more children's panels!

Astrid had already driven off to her next appointment, so Ruth and Morven had an ice cream at the bus station while waiting for the bus back to Flegg.

'Feels great,' said Ruth suddenly.

'Yeah,' Morven agreed. 'Aunt Ruth, when are we getting a dog?'

Jean-Luc was tidying up the forge after a hard day's work. Thibault had set off with the horses to deliver their newly shod charges back to their owners, and André was helping put away the tools and damp down the fire. They heard a bit of a commotion in the courtyard – hoofbeats, their father's voice and those of strangers – but by the time they got to the door of the shed, there was no-one in sight. Soon Thibault returned, and the three tired, hungry young men went into the house to eat their evening meal.

Their mother was stirring a pot on the fire, ready to dish it up into the waiting bowls. André's young wife, Isabelle, was laying out spoons while the baby snored in his cot by the fire. Pierre, their father, however, was sitting at the table with his arms folded, and a certain look on his face. 'What's the matter, Father?' asked Thibault.

'Is something wrong?' asked Jean-Luc.

'Let's just say I'm not used to having *letters* delivered,' replied Pierre. And he got up stiffly from the table and reached into the drawer of the dresser where they kept spare keys. He pulled out a scroll and brought it to the table, sitting down and placing it carefully in the middle for them all to behold.

Thibault and André whistled. 'Is it from the Abbey?' queried Thibault, 'I thought we had come to an agreement regarding that lame stallion. No cause for putting things in writing. It was his own fault anyway...'

'I saw the Abbot's ostler only yesterday,' said André, 'he mentioned nothing amiss.'

'What does it say on the front?' asked Thibault, and Jean-Luc stretched out his hand for a closer look, but his father's hand snatched it away before he could grab it.

'Who else?' he asked. 'None of the rest of us are grand enough for *letters*.' And his older two sons gazed at Jean-Luc in disbelief. 'For him?' said Thibault.

'*Ma foi!* Who is *he* getting letters from?' asked André.

'Let's just wait and find out,' said their father, handing the scroll over at last to Jean-Luc, who looked at it in consternation. 'Maybe it's another one from brother Joseph,' he said, 'but it doesn't look like his style. I thought I'd heard the last from him.'

'Well, what's he after this time?' grumbled his mother. She wasn't at all pleased at the tone Brother Joseph had taken in that last letter to her youngest son. Not that Jean-Luc had divulged every detail of the letter, but she had caught the tone of it and was most offended.

Jean-Luc broke the seal and unrolled the scroll, laying it flat out on the table. Everyone jostled to lean over and look at it, but he was the only one who could read it. It took him by surprise, as he deciphered the unusual style:

Dear Jean-Luc,

as you see I write with my own hand.

I am happy to hear from you. But do not ask me to come to France. It is too far, and I need to be close to my family. You must come and meet Archie and Fiona, and decide whether your home is in Scotland.

I remember you fondly,

Mairi

'Come on then, Jean-Luc,' urged Thibault, 'read it out!' But Jean-Luc had paused, his face scarlet. *'Qu'est-ce qu'il y a?'* said his father, 'Come on, we're all eager to know!'

'Who's it from anyway?' asked André. Even his mother had paused in laying out the meal and come to the table to peer over the unusual object on her kitchen table. Jean-Luc looked shocked. 'Tell him to spit it out, Pierre,' said his mother, 'It can't be that bad!'

'Oh well,' said Jean-Luc, 'I will read it out to you, but I think I'll have to explain some of its meaning to you.'

'We're not stupid, you know,' said Thibault.

'It's not that...,' said Jean-Luc, 'Anyway here goes...' Mumbling a little, he read the letter out exactly as written. There was a silence.

'What?' said his mother at last. 'Can girls read and write in Scotland?'

'Not many,' said Jean-Luc. 'Mairi is...'

'Well I think we can see who Mairi is,' said Thibault, always one to cut to the chase, 'but what is she saying? Who are Archie and Fiona?'

Jean-Luc bit his lip. 'I think they must be my children,' he said.

The commotion in the kitchen lasted for a good ten minutes, and Jean-Luc's mother eventually had to reheat the stew, gone cold in the bowls. There was a muted debate as to whether Scotland should allow girls to read and write, Jean-Luc meanwhile asking himself whether it could possibly be his Mairi, writing to him 'in her own hand.' There were questions as to the wisdom of sending letters off without being sure whether they would reach their intended recipient. Eventually, however, as rumbling stomachs were assuaged and anxieties faced, the main issue was broached, as Jean-Luc had known it would be: *how could you have babies and not know about it?* His mother had an acid edge of disgust in her voice, young Isabelle nodded vigorous agreement, and Jean-Luc was heartily ashamed. 'You must go to her straightaway,' said his father 'but how I wish you had told us about this. I am most disappointed in you. No wonder Brother Joseph was angry.'

'But,' said Thibault, 'she says she doesn't want to come to France. What's all that about?'

At last Jean-Luc found his voice. 'I thought you would all be pleased to meet her, and make her welcome, and I didn't know about the children myself until Joseph told me in his last letter. Actually, I thought it was only one child. So, I told her to come over here, and I would meet her at Calais. I sent her some money to pay the ferryman.'

Thibault repeated, 'But she says she doesn't want to come!'

'You knew about the babies all along!' shrieked his mother.

'And you invited her to come and live here without even telling us?' His father was aghast.

'Well, of course they must come here!' his mother rounded on his father. 'But some warning would be a good thing!'

'She says she doesn't want to come to France,' repeated Thibault. André and Isabelle listened and supped and waited for the return of order.

'I know,' said Jean-Luc, 'I didn't expect that.'

'Why ever not?' asked his father.

'Well, naturally she wants to be near her mother,' said his own mother, 'and you couldn't expect her to come with two little babies on such a long journey, unaccompanied – the very idea of it! Honestly, you young men! And old ones! Pierre, you're just as bad as him. You just don't think about things properly, do you?' There was a silence, and eventually his mother said there was pudding, and she banged a dish of poached pears down on the table, alongside a bowl of fermented sheep's milk. They took up their spoons and quietly supped, wondering what to make of all this. Jean-Luc was perturbed, and suddenly not at all hungry.

'I'll just go back to Scotland myself,' he said, 'I'm sorry to have upset you all.'

'I'll go with you,' said Thibault suddenly.

'Not so fast,' said his father, 'just eat your dinner and we will discuss it in the morning. And no sneaking away in the middle of the night either!' he warned, waving his spoon at Jean-Luc, 'This time, we work as a family!'

. . .

TWO DAYS LATER, A SMALL PROCESSION OF HORSES LEFT THE forge in the direction of Calais. Jean-Luc's father sat comfortably atop the first steed, while Jean-Luc came behind sitting on a fine chestnut mare, leading another horse which was laden with panniers. Jean-Luc's mother waved them off vigorously, shouting at them not to forget the gifts for the twins, especially the fine warm woollen shawls she had produced to keep them cosy on their journey back. André and Thibault waved briefly before heading to the forge – they would have it all their own way for the next few weeks, while their father and brother were away doing business in Scotland, and André relished the opportunity while Thibault pined to be away on the journey. But as Pierre had pointed out, they couldn't keep the forge running with only one man present, and the old man had surprised them all with his determination to go on this journey himself. André hoped Isabelle would be able to break the ice with this Mairi whom Jean-Luc was bringing back from Scotland. That would make up for his disappointment that their son's place as the only grandchild had been so quickly edged aside. As they all realised, life at the forge would not be dull for the foreseeable future. That younger brother of theirs! Forever getting into hot water! Admiration and annoyance chased each other round the family, as had always been the case with the youngest and his frequent scrapes. But this was more than a scrape, and as their father said, they would all need to work together.

The weather was settled and bright as Jean-Luc and his father embarked on a ferry bound for St Andrews. As the boat headed out into the open sea, Jean-Luc remembered with a lurch exactly how seasick he had been the last time he headed north on an open ship. He had tried to warn his father the night before, and suggested some moderation at their last dinner in France. However, Pierre – on what he felt was his first adventure in a lifetime – was not to be dissuaded from a massive bowl of mussels in fine Normandy cream and cider, helped down with the innkeeper's magnificent *canard confit* and a loaf of bread. 'Call me Pierre,' he had bidden their host as they were shown where to tie up the horses, and the Landlord and Pierre were soon the best of friends.

Pierre had pronounced the meal, the drinks, the company most satisfying; by the time they went to bed, he had convinced himself that this entire trip was his own idea, and the best he had ever had. 'I wonder how your mother would take to living by the sea?' he murmured as he dropped off to sleep. Jean-Luc, similarly provendered, was already snoring.

Aboard their ship they found that the sea, by its normal standards, was not at all choppy, nevertheless, the breeze stiffened as the shore faded into the distance. There were several passengers aboard who looked on in amused contempt as Jean-Luc and his father leant, retching, over the sides of their ship. Country men, apparently; presumably neither of them had travelled much. But Pierre and Jean-Luc simply did not believe their legs were made for pitching and tossing on a shifting ocean. Many anguished prayers were uttered before they fetched up at the quay at St Andrews, and the two men came staggering off, leading the flighty horses.

'Where is this place, anyway?' rasped his father.

Jean-Luc wearily replied, 'It's St Andrews. Named after the saint. Over there...,' and he pointed, 'That's where I threw up the last time…' And his father did likewise, his tall bulky frame only a little more bent than his son's.

'St. Andrews?' eventually his father processed the message. 'They have the same saints as us, in this godforsaken place?' He was relieved at least that the ground was no longer moving beneath his feet. 'Aye,' said Jean-Luc wearily, 'I did warn you about all those mussels.'

'Just give me ten minutes and I'll be fine,' said his father. And perhaps twenty minutes later, he was as good as his word. They found a tavern and drank some ale and ate some bread, and soon they were fit for the road again. As they cantered along, Jean-Luc acquainted his father with the rudiments of the English language. He laughed to hear the clumsy errors his father made; and recognised himself in his father, his father in himself. It had never occurred to Jean-Luc before that he resembled his father so closely; André was always the clever one, and Thibault the diplomat. Neither of them, however, had ever been half as good as Jean-Luc at the tools and the forge. For the first time he wondered whether they had been wise in leaving his brothers in charge; however, it would only be a short break, and they would be back in France before André and Thibault could do too much damage. 'How long till we get where we're going?' asked his father, and Jean-Luc calculated that it would probably be another six hours. Possibly the sun would be going down by the time they reached Flegg. 'Maybe we could stay with Arthur for the night,' he suggested, 'you know father, I told you about Arthur, the Flegg blacksmith? I was working with him before the Abbey was sacked, because he looked after all the Abbot's horses…'

'Excellent idea,' said his father, 'I'm looking forward to

meeting him.' And they trotted onwards, Pierre's fascination with his journey, and frequent questions, keeping Jean-Luc's mind off the forthcoming meeting with Mairi. Suddenly he felt less confident of their future together. He wondered whether to try and send a message ahead of them to alert her that they were on their way. He decided against it, his habitual optimism reasserting itself. They would be there soon enough. Perhaps Martin-Morven would be available to assist if required. Although, of course Pierre would find her too strange entirely. But she owed him three silver coins.

And anyway – what could possibly go wrong?

CHAPTER TWENTY-THREE

For October, it was unusually warm and dry. On the hills above Arbroath, the lightest of winds played across the grass: not enough to blow your paper away and be a nuisance, but just enough to move the trees a little, and ripple through the grass, and make the painting of the scene tantalisingly tricky. Hunkered down on a bench with their backs against an ancient oak tree, Aunt Linda and Morven were enjoying the vista.

'Well, you did say you wanted to find out how to be an artist!' laughed Aunt Linda. 'This is it – out in the cold, freezing your bum off and catching the moment.'

Morven laughed back. 'This is great,' she said, 'just like those students we saw that first time Aunt Ruth and I visited you here.'

'The land and seascapes are there for everybody to capture, in whatever way they want,' said Aunt Linda. 'It doesn't cost a penny. And we're lucky in Scotland to have some great views. If you lived for a hundred years you couldn't capture them all. How are you getting on with your drawing?' And she leaned over to have a look.

'I'm all out with the perspective,' frowned Morven, 'I've made this tree on the left too big, and there isn't room for that little boat out on the horizon, which was what I wanted the whole picture to be about. It's really difficult,' she complained.

'Recognising where you've gone wrong is more than half the battle,' said Aunt Linda. 'Just rub it out and start again. Is it time for the picnic yet?'

'No Aunt Linda! Just a little longer!' Linda sighed and laughed. Morven had never known an adult with such an appetite, and it was their little joke.

'Do you think Ruth's fed up shopping yet?' asked Aunt Linda.

'No way, all those charity shops? She could be there all day.'

'Oh well, hopefully she'll have had her fill by the time we meet up.'

It was the start of the October holidays, and Ruth and Morven were spending a few days with Linda in Arbroath. Linda was teaching Morven how to be an artist; they had acknowledged that she may or may not be able to put in the formal effort at school, for the necessary qualifications to go on to art school. But they weren't going to let her anxieties about Maths and English get in the way of being her own creative self, and developing her skills. Morven realised, not for the first time, that she was lucky to have discovered an aunt like Linda. Who would've thought they had artists in the family? A family like hers? Neither Jennifer nor Kyle had artists in their families, and neither did anybody else that she knew personally. It was better than discovering you had a rich uncle who would leave you money when he died – money could only take you so far, as Linda had told her, but artistic talent and commitment could take you to the ends of the earth.

Later that afternoon, as planned, they met up with Ruth in a cafe in the High Street. Coffee, hot chocolate and scones were ordered, and they shared their morning's news with each other. Morven's cheeks were pink and her eyes were sparkling, as were Linda's. 'Did you enjoy your shopping?' queried Linda.

Ruth laughed gratefully. 'It was fantastic!' she said, 'What a great array of thrift shops you've got here. It was lovely having time to browse around on my own and take my time... and not have you getting all impatient, Morven! I got some great bargains; I'll show you later.'

'Wait till you see our drawings!' said Morven. 'It was great up there on the hill. I felt like a real art student!'

'The main thing is having something to show for it,' said Linda. 'What are you doing for the rest of the school holidays? After you leave Arbroath?'

'Going to have a party, aren't we Morven?' said Ruth, 'And of course you're invited!'

'Wow, a party. What's the occasion?'

'It's to celebrate being finished with the children's hearing system, and Morven managing to settle down at school again so well, and me passing all my exams for the first term.'

'And also, to say how pleased we are to have you with us, in our lives,' added Morven, rather shyly.

'Brilliant!' said Linda. 'Who else is coming?'

'Kyle and his Dad, and Jennifer and her Mum and Dad, and Jade and Kate and… maybe somebody else?' and she looked at Ruth.

'Yes,' said Ruth, 'she texted me. She says she'll come for a little while, but she doesn't want to cramp our style. However, she said she wouldn't miss it for the world!'

Morven laughed and Aunt Linda asked, 'Who are we talking about?'

The other two voices came in unison, 'Astrid!' they chorused.

'The social worker?'

'Yes, the social worker,' said Ruth. 'I realised that she would probably enjoy seeing the good times as well as the bad.'

'Oh my! We'll have to be on our best behaviour!'

'She probably won't stay too long…'

'Well! That's good. What's the food going to be?' And they tossed various possibilities around as they ordered more scones.

CHAPTER TWENTY-FOUR

The young Richmond Douglas had made a decision. After a very short time, he could see that his marriage was going exactly the way his family had planned, and in most ways, it was acceptable to him – except in that one important particular.

He decided, after much scratching of his head, that he would have to explain this to Mairi. Most women in her position, he had presumed, would be grateful for the attentions of a young landowner and heir to a family fortune. She, however, did not appear to be ready to jump unquestioningly into his arms. This was puzzling, but he could not but be impressed at her intelligence and wit: partly in the putting together of the complicated letters which drove him to distraction, but also more generally, in the assertive way with which she dealt with her world. Here was no craven lackey, grateful for the few crumbs thrown from the master's table. What he had seen of her down that quarry, nearly two years ago now, had been Mairi at her best: sure-footed, focused, and determined. Childless. Every conversation he had snatched with her since then had confirmed him in his first impressions, except that he now had lots of other adjectives to describe her with: beautiful, elegant, graceful, gracious. Poor. Mother of twins.

Probably his wife would never bear him children of his own.

Really, Richmond reflected sadly, this world was not well arranged for his happiness. No matter how beautiful and talented this young woman was, she would never be considered an appropriate wife for him. How intensely cruel. He had worked out what he hoped was a reasonable alternative – and was now setting out to put it to her.

He rode over the hill from his father's house, having departed Dundee early that morning, and called in on his father en-route. With his father's blessing, he arrived at the Glenmiglo estate gates. There was still some light in the sky, and he dismounted and waited with his horse by the stile at the back of Mairi's mother's cottage. He was familiar with her movements; every evening she took Archie and Fiona out for some fresh air before heading home and settling down for the night. This would be a good time to catch a word. And sure enough, soon she came stepping out, a babe in each arm, heading down the Strath.

'Mairi!' he addressed her, 'My lady!' Mairi was not displeased to see him; he often materialised at this time of the night, and to be honest, she rather enjoyed the attention. She gave him a smile and said, 'Let me just hand the babies over to my mother.' She and her suitor were soon seated on a grassy mound, out of sight of both the cottage and the Big House, enjoying the last of the evening sun.

Mairi drew her shawl around her. She could see that young Richmond was a little nervous; and wondered what was on his mind. Jean-Luc's failure to respond to her carefully-wrought letter was an ongoing disappointment to her, and she had begun to fear that her mother might be right – that she might never see him again. She decided to hear young Richmond out. Who knew what he might suggest? There might be some merit in it for her. And he wasn't such a dreadful prospect, surely? Many girls had husbands chosen for them, and barely even met them until their wedding days. Love, Jess had assured her, was something you hoped for, not something you could confidently expect. Her own experience demonstrated this abundantly; with little choice in taking a husband, Jess had been more or less gifted to Hugh when she was 14, and throughout their many years together, they had developed an understanding. Just that – an understanding. Jess believed in understandings. She had known of many marriages where understandings were not present, and, 'Believe me,' she would say to Mairi, 'I know which is best!'

'Best? An understanding where he beat you up whenever it pleased him?'

'You mind your lip, my girl!' Jess as usual felt misunderstood.

Richmond set out his argument, 'I want to explain to you my position, and exactly what I am offering you.' Mairi raised her eyebrows; this was interesting. 'I know you must wonder at me, leaving a new wife behind to come courting.' And she nodded. 'And furthermore, I am aware that in this world which sets value on the wrong things, you and I could never be blessed in a proper union. How I wish that might be different!' Mairi coloured up a little, but gave him her full attention, keeping her counsel.

'My new wife,' he continued, 'is my full cousin. She is a widow, some years older than me, with two small sons of her own. Last year her husband was killed in a hunting accident, and now she is dependent on his parents for everything. My aunt and uncle are somewhat at the end of their resources; and it has been agreed between her parents and mine that we could profitably combine our estates and in this way, rescue my cousin from penury while strengthening both our estates. She is a good woman, and I wish her no harm at all. But I cannot say that there is much desire in our marriage for... for a... a deeper intimacy.' And he paused, blushing, raising his eyes to meet Mairi's. 'I believe she is still in grieving for her fine young husband, and that she no more desires this arrangement than I do. Still, we are both aware of our duties to our respective parents; and of course, to her children.

'And meantime you, madam, have quite stolen my heart. I cannot give you what a woman of your abilities should command. But I would set you up in a fine home, in one of my father's mansions in Perth, with servants as required, and completely at your disposal. Of course, you would bring your babies, and I would visit as often as I possibly could.'

He reached out and took her hand, and somewhat stunned, she allowed this. 'This is not the ideal that I would wish for; but I truly believe it could make us both happy. At least,' he stammered, 'I know it would make me very happy, and I hope it would you too.

'I don't expect you to say yes or no right now. But please do not suffer me to wait too long.' He held her eyes, searching for assent, or willingness, or best of all joy. But he could not quite put a name to the emotion he read in those green depths. Shock was evident, but what else? He sighed and stood, 'Madam, I bid you good night. I will visit again in a week's time, and hear your decision on this matter.' He mounted his fine black stallion, pausing before digging his heels in. 'It's a good offer,' he threw at her, 'I don't suppose you'll get another like it.' He set off, riding back down the Strath in the direction of Dundee. So – he was going straight back to his wife.

Mairi sat for another five minutes alone on the grass, trying to absorb what had just happened, and remember the details of the remarkable offer Richmond had just made her. She was in shock, and couldn't put a name to her emotions. Was she pleased at what he had said? Would it be a good outcome for her? More to the point, was there anything better on the horizon? What if he grew tired of her? But then, what else did she have to hope for? Would she regret passing up such a chance on the basis of an untried promise from her erstwhile lover, far away in France, a man whom she had to accept that she hardly knew? Her mother's views on love and understandings came to her. And the harsh reality that, having borne children out of wedlock, marriage was unlikely to come her way.

Richmond Douglas wasn't proposing marriage to her, that was the difficulty. Mairi would never have the dignity of her own legitimate and acknowledged place as Mrs Anything, if she accepted his offer – whereas the shunned wife was probably Lady Douglas or some such. On the other hand, Mairi could well imagine her mother's ecstasy at the prospect of her daughter being set up in a comfortable mansion in Perth, with servants and everything that she needed. And yes, it was an enticing proposition for a poor girl. So why did she hesitate?

She remembered all the effort she had put in to her literacy. She was better at reading and writing than he was. And the arrogance of his final words had not escaped her. She stood up and shook her apron and gown, and wrapping herself tightly in her shawl, returned to the stile, stepped over and back to her mundane normal life. Time to greet her mother, feed the twins, and go to bed. Later on, she would shake out the little letters and see whether there was any wisdom to be had.

'What did the young Douglas want?' her mother demanded, but Mairi could not repeat just yet what he had said to her. 'Oh, nothing much,' she replied.

Jess was prepared to be patient. 'Well don't keep him waiting then,' she said in a matter-of-fact manner, going back to sweeping the kitchen floor. Having found a potential solution to her daughter's disgrace and certain impoverishment, she was happy to wait till the young nobleman decided the time was right. No point in fussing at things over which you have no control.

In Flegg, the young Douglas headed for the last evening ferry for Dundee. He wasn't to know that the two jolly strangers riding into town, leading a laden pony behind them, had anything at all to do with his romantic fortunes. And neither did Jean-Luc and his father have any notion at all that this young nobleman, confidently mounted on his fine stallion, had anything at all to do with theirs. The travellers nodded at each other in the passing, and went on their way – young Richmond down to the ferry, and Jean-Luc and his father up the hill to the home of Arthur, the village blacksmith. Jean-Luc paused – should he leave his father with Arthur, and canter on up the hill, catching Mairi by surprise? But it was already darkening and so he decided to leave it till the next day. He lifted the latch on Arthur's gate.

Up the hill, Mairi put her babies to bed, lit her candle and shook out the little pouch of letters, searching for wisdom.

CHAPTER TWENTY-FIVE

The night before the party, Morven was tidying up her bedroom to make way for the camp bed; it had been agreed that Jade would stay for a sleepover after the party, although in a final show of bureaucracy, Astrid had insisted that there would need to be a full risk assessment before this could be allowed. Rather than go through the irritation of an argument, or the even bigger irritation of having to fill in all the forms, Ruth had just said, 'Oh well, we'll let it drop for now.' The question of whether or not Jade would be allowed to stay had been quietly shelved, and up till now, Morven and Jade had thought it wasn't going to happen. However, Aunt Ruth had just confessed to Morven that she and Kate had conspired together, and there would be an overnight bag in Kate's car for Jade, which would be kept hidden until Astrid had left the party. 'Aunt Ruth!' Morven had gasped in mock horror. 'You mean you're telling lies to the social worker?'

'Not really lies, Morven,' laughed Ruth, 'Nobody is going

to come to any harm, and you and Jade will have a lot of fun together.'

So, this meant digging in corners of her bedroom for the dirty socks that never made it to the laundry basket, and running the hoover around, and looking out clean sheets. As she was picking things up off the carpet to stop them being sucked into the hoover, Morven found some of the little metal letters from her collection. She held them in her palm with her other hand over them, exactly the same way she had that very first time at the Labyrinth, and soon she felt the familiar warming and vibrating sensation. She sat down quietly on the edge of her bed and closed her eyes.

There she was, the auburn beauty, sitting on the branch of a tree, wearing a long white dress with her usual woollen shawl around her shoulders. The dress was different from usual – normally it was an old patched skirt and big apron that M wore. Today however, must be special - there were flowers in her hair, in a beautiful woven coronet. For the first time, Morven also spied two other girls, also with long red hair just like her own, in blue dresses with clean white aprons, and clutching little posies of flowers. They sat on another limb of the tree a little higher up; and the three of them gazed down into the meadow below, as if watching some tournament. What were they watching?

As Morven sat there with her eyes closed, she saw a procession of three men riding on horseback into the arena. They halted below M's branch, and the man in the middle, wearing a fine cloak and strong leather boots, looked up and addressed her. 'Here you are then Madam,' called the man, 'Which will you choose?' And on his right hand was a young blonde youth, expensively dressed, leading a chestnut mare, and on the other hand – Morven gasped – it was Merlin, the beautiful black stallion from down the field on the way out of Flegg. On his broad back sat Jean-Luc, her friend from the Labyrinth.

'Choose Jean-Luc! Choose Jean-Luc!' shouted Morven, desperate to make her voice heard through the centuries.

Ruth's voice came floating up the stairs. 'What's going on up there?'

'Nothing, just tidying up.' But she kept her eyes closed and her hands clasped around the letters as long as she could make the vision last, willing her great great great great-for-ever grandmother to choose a good man – a man whom Morven knew to be a strong friend.

Slowly the vision faded, before Morven could be sure which choice M would make. But she sat there anyway, on the side of her bed, silently praying that of all the mysterious men in her family, she might yet discover that she was descended from the one who had been a strong friend to her, just when she needed him.

CHAPTER TWENTY-SIX

Earl Maxwell Douglas had taken a ride over the hills to consult with Sir Peter, accompanying his two sons on their weekly reading and writing trip. While they sat in class with Brother Joseph, somewhat bored and not working very hard, Sir Peter took the Earl for a stroll around his orchard, and soon enough Earl Douglas broached the matter which had brought him here.

'... The boy has been very patient about the marriage,' he explained, 'and being the younger of the two, recognises his duty. Our niece is a sensible girl, but we can all see that young Richmond will need to have his own opportunities as well.'

Sir Peter nodded in agreement. 'Yes, I can quite see that,' he said, 'and plenty young men in his position have managed to find their pleasures as well as do their duty; without causing anyone any harm.'

'So, I wanted to know what you think of his proposed liaison with this young woman from your estate? Richmond seems quite fixed on her,' said the Earl. 'No prospects of her own, I take it?'

'None whatsoever,' said Sir Peter, 'but then your Richmond isn't looking for marriage, is he – being married already? You wouldn't be expecting someone with *prospects*?'

'Just making sure she isn't promised to someone else, who might make trouble. I just wondered what you knew of the girl and her family.'

'You probably met her father,' said Sir Peter, 'my steward, Hugh, the one who fell down the quarry last year and was killed outright?'

'Oh yes, I remember him,' said the Earl. 'Not a great one for progress, was he?'

'That would be an understatement,' laughed Sir Peter. 'He really didn't see the point of the orchard or any of the innovations that the monks have shown us, and he could be downright obstinate at times. On the other hand, he was a hard worker and loyal, and his family have been tenants of ours for generations; they were all faithful servants in their way. His father and grandfather before him – I remember my own father valued them highly.'

'And the girl?'

'Very clever, apparently,' said Sir Peter. 'Brother Joseph doesn't want to admit it, but she appears to be the star in his reading and writing class. I will admit I did not want her in the class at all – it seemed quite inappropriate – but she was very keen. So, Joseph let her sit in at the back. Behind a screen.'

'My goodness! A young lass reading and writing? Whatever for?'

'A notion she took. I suppose she has inherited some of

her father's stubbornness. And I'm sorry to say… notwithstanding your own two sons, and also my young Patrick, it seems she outshines all her classmates!'

'Never!'

'She is helping brother Rodriguez put together the print frames for the orchard book, and apparently she is very neat in her habits and meticulous in the way that she goes about her work. The book is coming along quite nicely, with her assistance.'

'My, my!' said the Earl, 'How unusual! Can she keep house?'

'Yes, I should think so,' said Sir Peter. 'Of course, she has the two babes to consider.'

'Ah yes. I heard about them.'

'Otherwise I expect she might have found a mate hereabouts.' The two men shrugged; not an unusual story.

'And do you think she has the capacity to handle money, and keep staff in their place?'

'I don't imagine she has any experience of those things,' said Sir Peter, curiosity kindling in his eyes. 'Although my wife says she's a good girl and often organises the younger staff. Why do you ask?'

'I'm just trying to make sure my son doesn't make a terrible mistake.'

Sir Peter shared this conversation, later that night, with Lady Janet, as they sipped a glass of wine together before bedtime. Lady Janet was intrigued. 'My goodness,' she said, 'young Richmond must be planning to make some kind of an offer to young Mairi.' And the next day, she dropped a little hint to Jess as she was working in the dairy. 'What was that?' said Jess, not sure she was hearing right.

'Keep it quiet for now,' said Lady Janet, 'but Earl Douglas was consulting with Sir Peter about whether your Mairi would be a suitable housekeeper for him.'

'Housekeeper? For the Earl?'

'Well I'm not entirely sure. Don't say anything to Mairi just now, it's probably not decided yet. Probably not for the Earl,' she added, 'for the young son I expect.'

Jess went home that night in a ferment of excitement, and was waiting for Mairi when she brought the twins down at supper time. 'Young Richmond is going to make you an offer!' she said. 'His father was asking about you!'

Mairi started. 'What did he want to know?' she asked.

'I've no idea,' said Jess. 'Anyway – just you be on your best behaviour, and make sure you're looking your best for the next little while. This could be a great result for the family! Your father would be so proud!'

Mairi opened her mouth to point out that her father would probably have been quite obstinate about the whole suggestion. And also, she thought to point out, the only reason young Douglas had started calling on her in the first place, was that he had helped her pull her father's dead body out of the quarry. And furthermore, she reflected, she could give her mother a whole lot more information about exactly what the young Douglas was offering, if she chose. None of this seemed quite right however, so she said nothing.

And still, she remembered, with a bitter twist in her heart – no reply to her letter.

Pierre and Arthur, down in the village smiddy, were getting on like a house on fire. Neither of the men had many opportunities to discuss the finer points of blacksmithing with others who understood the complexities; it was wonderful for them both to have someone to appreciate their skills. Jean-Luc was anxious to get away from them and up the hill to find Mairi, but Pierre as yet was finding it tricky to understand the English language, and held Jean-Luc back. Arthur had been delighted to welcome them in, and his wife Kate had reluctantly bid them stay the night. When she got her husband on his own however, she demanded to know what he was thinking of, 'I thought you wanted that young man for your niece?'

'Well yes, I do... or at least I would like...'

'Are you blind as well as stupid? Don't you see he's planning to get back up to Glenmiglo, to see that young one of the steward's? It must be his babies she's been parading around.'

Arthur winced at the spite in his wife's voice. 'Well I don't know how it'll all turn out,' he said. 'I don't know if they are his babies or not.' Then he remembered that he did know – that Jean-Luc had in fact confessed as much. But there was no need for his wife to have further ammunition. 'We can't stop him going to see her. If they have anything to say to each other, let them say it. It's none of our business. But I'm pleased to welcome him and his father here – you probably don't realise what good blacksmiths they are. It's wonderful to hear them talk about how they do things in France! I would love to see it with my own eyes... We'll see what my niece says the next time she calls. Just don't you go tittle-tattling all around the place.'

'The factor's wife says...' started Kate.

'And how do you know what the factor's wife says?' demanded Arthur.

'Well my friend Agnes, Mrs Cunningham's housekeeper, says the family is no better than it should be. She has one of the young twins with her now, the steward's younger daughter.'

'And is she a good girl?'

'I don't think there are any complaints in that respect,' sniffed Kate.

'I won't have gossip!' said Arthur. 'We will be hospitable to our guests and that's the end of it, do you hear me?'

'As you say,' she muttered, her lips pressed close together.

LATER THAT EVENING, JEAN-LUC SLIPPED AWAY FROM THE blacksmith's fireside, leaving Pierre and Arthur happily engaged in a debate about anvils, much ale having already disappeared down their throats. Ale improved Pierre's English enormously, and even had an impact on Arthur's French. The two men were in perfect accord, united by a fast-evolving Franco-Scottish language of gestures. They didn't need Jean-Luc by that time. He led the chestnut mare from the stable, and they set off up the fondly remembered hill to Glenmiglo. Unlike the young Douglas, Jean-Luc was in no position to know what Mairi's evening routines might be; he presumed that the day's work was over, and expected to find her at her mother's cottage. Sure enough, as he turned up the hill at the blasted oak tree – still full of bees, he noted – he saw her in the distance: a tall strong young woman, her blaze of auburn hair wafting in the wind, carrying a small child on either hip – and quite heavy they must be, he realised. Full of awe for the extra work he had so unthinkingly caused her, he hastened up the path to meet her.

Mairi heard the hoof beats and looked up, wondering whether young Douglas had returned earlier than promised; she had thought herself to have another week before she would have to give him an answer. The sun was in her eyes as it dipped towards the horizon and she couldn't quite make out the identity of the rider or the horse. Thank goodness, it wasn't Richmond. But who was it? The outline was familiar – that bulk, the way of sitting on the horse. She stood still and adjusted the twins as she tried to make out the face of the person ahead of her. Surely it couldn't be him, whose return she had awaited with such ardour? Surely not.

Jean-Luc heaved himself off the horse, and bid it wait for him while he stepped forward to reveal himself to Mairi. Suddenly he felt anxious. Maybe she wouldn't want him after all? After he had left her with such a pair of challenges on her hands?

And suddenly Mairi's stomach turned over. This was the man she hardly knew: the man with whom she had frolicked in the barn, whose babies she had faithfully loved and tended, and who looked to her alone for their very survival.

What if they had made a huge mistake? What if they didn't like each other after all? He removed his cap, and stood nervously fingering it. She had forgotten how handsome he was!

'Well!' she found her voice, 'You took your time.'

CHAPTER TWENTY-SEVEN

Morven couldn't sleep that night. She heard the Steeple bell chime midnight and crept from her bed to gaze out of the window. The moon was full, the town bathed in a gentle silver light. Morven couldn't get her great great great etc Grandmother M out of her mind. It looked, from that last vision, as if M was having to choose between two men – probably for a husband given the white gown and the flowers in her hair. It was like a fairy story. In Morven's own life, she knew nothing of girls and boys pairing off and having fairy-tale weddings together. She had seen her mother's succession of lovers come and go, each one worse than the one before – if that's what the word 'lover' meant, Morven didn't want any of them. Then of course there was that visit from someone called Uncle Gordon, who to her astonishment had turned out to be Aunt Ruth's ex-husband. That had been a shocker. Ruth wouldn't talk about him, but he had looked decent enough, and Morven had the unsettling feeling that maybe Aunt Ruth had been sad about the end of their marriage. She felt obscurely responsible.

Would she herself ever want to settle down with someone? In her class of thirty youngsters, there were a couple of girls who regarded themselves as madly in love and planning their future weddings. They were an out-and-out mystery to Morven, and a source of intense fascination to all the other girls in the class. Then there was another half-dozen or so who seemed to not find the idea of having a boyfriend or girlfriend too abhorrent, and who circulated around a bit, pairing up and then breaking up again in short order. It was a mystery to Morven and she didn't really want to know about it. But it was different in 'the olden days,' as she learned from the telly. She wondered what it must mean to M, all those centuries ago, having two men, both apparently wanting to marry her. What was that all about?

She was wide awake now, and Aunt Ruth was fast asleep in the room next door. The silvery night looked so inviting. She could be back long before Aunt Ruth had even noticed she was gone. While these thoughts drifted through her head, she had absently reached for her T-shirt and jeans and socks, and by the time she had made her decision to slip out into the night, found she was already fully dressed. Inch by inch, not wanting to make the slightest creak or rustle, she edged her way past Aunt Ruth's bedroom door, down the stairs, and out by the back door, grabbing her anorak and trainers as she went. She did a couple of star jumps on the grass, just for the joy of being out there, and set off at a fast lope. Her trainers padded silently on the tarmac as she legged it down the main road and out through the eastern end of Flegg.

Merlin waited for her by the edge of his field; he must have known she was on her way. She gave him a quick scratch of the nose and a hug, and quickly jumped up onto his back, nudged him with her knees, and they were off up the hill to Glenmiglo, Merlin sure of the way.

MAIRI, BETH AND PEGGY WERE MAKING THEMSELVES comfortable in the wide low branches of an ancient oak tree a hundred yards or so from Jess's cottage. The night was cool as well as silvery, and Mairi had brought extra blankets from home for the consultation. Little Archie and Fiona were tucked into a pile of hay together at the foot of the tree, well within Mairi's line of sight; they slept deeply.

'So,' said Peggy, 'what did you want to see us about?'

'Shhh!' Mairi held her hand up, 'Listen?' And they all looked out and saw a rider on a black horse canter into view and then pull up silently below their tree. Mairi smiled down, recognising her immediately. She reached down and held out her hand. 'Thank you for coming. Come on up and join us; this is the best way – get your foot in that low branch.' And in a few seconds, Morven was perching up among the branches beside them. They looked round at each other; four redheads – each of them somewhere on a spectrum between auburn and ginger – all within a few years in age, all with curiosity written large over their open faces. But it was obvious that Mairi was the one in charge, and having issued Morven, the youngest, with a blanket and made the introductions, she addressed her little gathering.

'I need your help,' she announced. The others stirred and fidgeted a little. Mairi continued, 'I think we've all seen women being unhappy through various difficulties in their lives, and I would like us all to learn to make good choices. Not just me – although it's very urgent for me at the moment – but all of us. We need to get better at choosing the right thing, and not just putting up with the choices other people make for us Or, choosing the right man.'

'Is this about the young Douglas?' asked Beth, beginning to giggle.

'Or Jean-Luc?' asked Peggy, snorting out loud – and Morven knew at once what the issue was.

'Choose Jean-Luc!' she said, urgently.

'No, choose the Douglas!' said Beth.

'Which one do you want to choose?' asked Peggy.

Mairi grimaced. 'That's the problem,' she said, 'I don't know how to choose. And stop giggling, you pair! This is important!'

'It's called criteria,' said Morven, and the others stared at her in puzzlement, 'Criteria,' Morven repeated, 'we're doing it at school.'

'School?' Beth and Peggy chorused.

'Yes, in second year,' said Morven, 'you figure out what you really want, and that's called criteria, and then you line your options up against them and give them points out of ten.'

'My goodness,' they muttered among themselves. Mairi addressed Morven, 'This is why I wanted you here tonight. You are so much cleverer than we are, I think, all those years in the future. I bet you're really good reading and writing?'

Morven shrugged. 'Well, not really,' she considered, 'most of the people in my class are better, and I'm not all that great at counting either. But I'm good at drawing.'

'You don't know how lucky you are!' And Mairi turned to her younger sisters, 'Never forget this! In years to come, every girl in the land will be able to read and write! Think what a difference that will make to us!'

Morven's heart was beating fast. She had never spoken out like that in her life before, but this, she saw, was family. She didn't want to deceive them though, to let them think she was anything special. 'I'm not all that clever,' she said, 'I've made loads of mistakes. But let me just ask this – are you telling me that girls don't get to read and write in your time?'

'Most boys don't either,' said Peggy, 'Mairi's got a bee in her bonnet.'

'That's enough,' said Mairi, 'we haven't got all night. Mother will be awake in a couple of hours, and Morven has to get back down to Flegg, and you two have to get back up the Strath before you're missed. That word CRITERIA you mentioned, Morven. And 'scoring points out of ten' – how do we do that?'

'You decide what you want, ideally, as your outcome – that's the thing you want to end up with. And then you look at your options and see how they match up. So, let's say you want money to be an outcome, you then look at Options A, B, and so on, and give them points out of ten for how much money each would bring... and of course it's not just about money, you can choose any kind of criteria.'

'Such as?'

'Well, love I suppose – whether you fancy them or not. Or maybe, I don't know...' Morven's imagination wasn't up to guessing how girls might choose a partner. 'Looks?'

The others were paying close attention, nodding. Yes,

they could see the sense of what she was saying. 'All right then,' said Mairi. 'Help me figure out criteria for the choice I have to make. Morven, can you keep score please, since you're the best at reading and writing.' Morven complied, although she still couldn't quite believe she was the best in any kind of school subject. They broke some dead twigs off the tree and used them to score the various items they came up with. Absorbed in their task, they barely noticed as the sky began to glow in the east, down beyond Flegg. 'Look at that!' broke off Morven suddenly, 'I've got to go!'

'Gosh, us too!' and they all tumbled out of the tree together. 'Watch out for Fiona and Archie! Don't step on them!' whispered Mairi. They all hugged and promised to meet again, and Morven jumped on Merlin and sped down the hill and on towards the village while Beth whistled for a white mare that came cantering to take the two of them back up the Ninebells Road.

Mairi went home and wrote it all down, labouring with her letters till the sun came up. The criteria, the options, the scoring. It was most satisfying. She gave the little metal letters a gentle massage between her palms in gratitude for the appearance of her great-great-great-and so on Grand-daughter. And Morven felt it like a squeeze on the shoulder as she jumped back into bed and fell asleep. And Merlin felt it like a rub on the nose, back in his meadow, as he lay down under his favourite tree.

CHAPTER TWENTY-EIGHT

Brother Joseph had got hold of a copy of a book by his great enemy, John Knox. It had been published a few years ago, while the Queen was still in France, and was doubtless an argument against the possibility that she might ever return to Scotland to reign. However, despite its seditious content, brother Joseph had been unable to resist the title. 'The First Blast of the Trumpet against the Monstrous Regiment of Women,' it was called. How Joseph agreed with that sentiment! Not regarding the Queen of course; it was God's job to decide who might be on the throne, and he was glad not to be responsible for that. However, at a much more local level, ever since that girl had entered his classroom, he had been forced to put up with all kinds of challenges, and he found it most disagreeable.

His thoughts were interrupted by Rodriguez bursting into the chapel and seizing him by the sleeve: 'Guess what! Guess what...'

'Brother! Whatever is the matter?'

'There is to be a duel down at the Abbey ruins!' burst out Rodriguez. 'The young Douglas, and...'

'In the ruins? I'll have you know they are barely ruined yet! That is hallowed ground, there can be no such thing! I must see to this.' And he seized a bridle and went straight out to the stables. Brother Rodriguez pattered on behind him in his sandals, 'We should take the cart, Brother Joseph!' he cried, 'We must all come down and ... er, help you break it up ...'

'For goodness sake,' said Joseph, 'I'm not waiting for the cart – you bring it if you must.' And he raced on down the field on his horse. Rodriguez called for Anselm and together they yoked up and climbed aboard. As they were doing so, Sir Peter's coach came rattling out of the courtyard, his fine draught horses trotting briskly. Jess and Jean the Cook clung to the back of the coach, and they caught sight of Lady Janet and some of the children hanging on inside. Rodriguez and Anselm pulled in behind, and were just getting underway, when Jess's two small boys came rushing out, begging for a lift. On the road down to the Abbey, they came on a crowd of villagers, all running in the same direction. Joseph bustled impatiently past them, determined to get there first and put a stop to whatever nonsense was under way – all caution about being seen by Knox's men thrown to the winds.

He arrived at the foot of the hill under the Bear, dismounted and led his horse through the south entrance. There, to his fury, stood two young men on horseback, facing up to each other – the young Douglas! And of course, he might have known – who else but that disobedient lump Jean-Luc, who was supposed to be still in France.

'What the hell are you doing here? I told you to stay well

away!' He hurled at his erstwhile servant, and to the other young man, the local nobleman, he uttered 'Sir! This is not worthy of you! I beg you to refrain from...'

'Stand aside, monk!' snarled the young Douglas, his face scarlet and his whole body tensed for battle. But Joseph seized his horse's reins and tried to drag the horse and rider away from the sanctuary; meantime, shouting over his shoulder, 'As for you! You should know better than defile holy ground in this outrageous manner!'

Jean-Luc jumped down from his horse, and patted Merlin on the rump, so that the horse trotted obediently away to the side, out of harm's way. 'Let's leave the horses out of this!' he shouted at the young Douglas, meantime elbowing Joseph in the stomach so that the monk fell back, gasping. Reluctantly, Douglas dismounted; he had hoped to maintain advantage by hanging on to his fine chestnut mare, and had been quite taken by surprise when Jean-Luc turned up on such a prestigious mount. However, he would not shy away from his enemy's direct challenge, and so he took up his stance opposite, feet wide apart, knees bent, his weight gracefully balanced, his right hand resting on the hilt of his sword.

Jean-Luc, poised like a bear, raised both hands upwards in front of him and goaded the nobleman on. Meantime Joseph had regained his breath, and came lurching forward between them, determined not to allow the sacred ground of the Abbey to be despoiled by such unseemliness.

The first of the townsfolk were streaming into the Abbey courtyard, led by Arthur and Pierre. Behind them rattled the Glenmiglo cart, with Rodriguez and Anselm clinging aloft. They abandoned it in the roadway, and two little boys jumped out and came running into the field. Next came Sir Peter and Lady Janet, having more decorously guided their horse and coach to a neater halt a little further up the road. Their party dismounted and ran to join the others in the Abbey courtyard while yet more villagers piled onto the scene; and it became obvious to Jean-Luc and the young Douglas that their dispute was no longer a private matter. Quite unsought by them, it seemed that everyone from miles around had come to witness the battle for the hand of the fair Mairi. Everyone, that is, apart from Mairi herself.

Young Douglas found himself surrounded by supporters – some of whom he might have expected to be on his side, and others definitely not. Of course, there was Sir Peter and Lady Janet. But there also was Jess, his desired one's mother, and with her a younger sister whom she addressed as Peggy. His own father, The Earl Maxwell Douglas, had appeared as if from nowhere, along with the Factor Cunningham – how on earth does word get out so fast? Perhaps the Factor had brought Peggy, who as young Douglas now remembered was employed as a servant in the Factor's household.

As for Jean-Luc, who expected no support at all – there, of course, was his father. Thank goodness for fathers! But then he also caught sight of Mairi's younger sister Beth. And also, Rodriguez and Anselm, reluctantly holding Joseph back but definitely on his side.

The townspeople argued loudly about which of the suitors to support. A Frenchman? What a nerve! But a nobleman? Why should they always get it their own way? And the Frenchman was known to them, and had helped one or two of them out in the past... They gravitated to Jean-Luc's side of the battlefield.

Surprisingly, the Factor Cunningham strode backwards and forwards between the two groups. Even more surprisingly, and to Jean-Luc's and Pierre's disappointment, Arthur the blacksmith seemed torn in two directions. 'It's just,' he uttered painfully to Arthur, 'it's just that I would love the boy to marry my niece Sally, and work for me in the forge, and if there is someone else willing to take on that girl with her two babies, then so be it! It's a lucky break for Jean-Luc!' Pierre gazed at Arthur in astonishment, 'But they're coming back to France with me!'

All this commotion had elevated the battle to mythic status. It was no longer two suitors scrapping over the woman they loved: it was Scotland versus France, it was rich versus poor, it was honour or disgrace. Jean-Luc and Richmond were desperate to get at each other, but were being held back on all sides by hot advice. In the hiatus, Joseph managed to drive them all out by the Slype, so that the arena for the fight now became the absent Abbot's herbarium. This was the best he could do; probably it was a grey area in theological terms, but certainly less hallowed than the former Abbey itself.

The two young men threw off their entourage and faced up to each other again; young Douglas was grasping a fine sword, and Jean-Luc grasping a length of chain with a spiked iron ball at its end, borrowed from Arthur's forge. It was anyone's guess who might have won – the nobleman's fine training and proud weapon up against the commoner's fearless brutality.

Cunningham the factor strode into the space between them, and addressed not just them but the whole crowd, 'Which of you young men,' he addressed them almost as if they were equals,' which of you young men is going to ensure that the lady Mairi will continue to follow her scholarship?'

Jean-Luc and Richmond gazed at him in disbelief. What was he on about? Joseph shook his head in disgust. But Cunningham continued.

'Neither of you should imagine that by your strength alone you can determine the outcome of this battle! We have other good horses, fine swordsmen, even good blacksmiths in Scotland! There are other elements which are in short supply!'

'What is that to you, Sir?' flung Joseph, astounded at such sentiments. 'What do you hope to gain from all of this?'

'Brother, I am a merchant. I believe in trade. I believe in trading between nations, and the benefits that free trade will bring us all. You want us to read the Bible; well, maybe that will help too. I want to be able to write down a contract, and read a commission, and understand what my more literate enemies are planning against me!'

Joseph fell back open-mouthed. Cunningham turned back to the combatants.

'The lady's skills are as important to Scotland as your undoubted courage and valour!' Everybody looked at each other in confusion; none of the commoners dared to argue with the Factor, on whose approval so many of them depended. But what nonsense he appeared to be talking!

Peggy and Beth were whispering to each other and came to an agreement. They reached into a hastily-assembled bower of branches, and brought out Mairi's year-old twins, young Archie and Fiona. Both were now able to wriggle and crawl, though neither as yet were actually walking. Peggy and Beth brought the young babies to the space between the combatants, where the factor still held his position. Beth tugged at the Factor's sleeve and whispered to him at some length; and then he spoke up:

'I have a message from the lady who is the subject of this conflict. She wishes me to announce that one of her – ahem– *criteria* for deciding on a partner in life is that person's willingness as a parent.'

'They're mine!' bellowed Jean-Luc, 'I am their father and I will care for them!'

The young Douglas looked as if he were about to reply. His father, Earl Maxwell Douglas, stepped out to him and hissed, 'Leave it! Leave the field! I insist!' But young Douglas would not leave the field. 'And where have you been,' he screamed at Jean-Luc, 'all this time when she had no means of support? I can offer her so much more than you! In fact,' he added slyly, 'I already have!'

'Leave it!' snapped his father. The factor was pushed aside, and Beth and Peggy quickly seized their niece and nephew and retreated into the bower for safety, peeping out to try and see what was going on.

Young Douglas broke away from his father, dropping his sword. Jean-Luc dropped his chain and spike, and smacked Richmond a hefty blow on the shoulder. Richmond punched Jean-Luc in the jaw, and soon the two men were slugging it out among the Abbot's lavender and hyssop. They tussled and tore at each other, Richmond nimble and swift; Jean-Luc slow and deadly. Both were bloodied and gasping. The crowd roared in approval – this after all, was what they had come to watch. Eventually Jean-Luc managed to get Richmond down on the ground, and knelt clumsily on top of him, almost crushing the young man's ribs. At last, the thrashing of Douglas's limbs ceased; Jean-Luc was pulled off him, and Earl Maxwell Douglas knelt to ascertain the damage as his son groaned in agony. Jean-Luc was himself severely injured, one arm looking as if it had been jerked from its socket.

It seemed that Jean-Luc, last man standing, had won the fight. However young Peggy approached the Factor in the same way that her sister had earlier, pulled his sleeve and gave a further whispered message. The Factor looked askance, and made her repeat the message. Then he addressed the crowd, 'Ladies and gentlemen,' he announced, 'young Douglas and you, young Frenchman – I have to tell you that the girl Mairi regrets she is not at present willing to commit herself. She wishes to continue working on her book.' He smirked. 'You may as well go home.'

The crowd milled around, confused, and the young Douglas and Jean-Luc glared at each other. Their business wasn't finished yet.

CHAPTER TWENTY-NINE

Aunt Linda had told Ruth and Morven to expect a delivery on the morning of the party. 'But it's not anybody's birthday,' said Ruth, 'we don't need any presents.'

'It's not really a present for you and Morven, it's for the party itself. Wait and see. I think you'll like it. That's if the weather is fair anyway.'

The parcel was large and bulky, and the delivery man obviously was finding it very heavy as he manoeuvred it up the garden path at eight o'clock in the morning. 'What can it be?' asked Morven, jiggling around in her pyjamas, 'Can I open it?'

'Let me find the scissors...' And they fought their way past a forest of heavy cardboard and strong brass staples to reveal a huge iron half-dome – a fire pit. 'So, does this mean we can have the party outside?' asked Morven, and they went out to the garden to figure out the best arrangement.

The warm sunny October weather had continued, and

Ruth's back garden was well sheltered – but it would be cold after dark, and so the fire pit was the perfect solution. Soon after they had unwrapped it, Aunt Linda herself arrived, bringing various other contributions for the party – fairy lights and sausages. Their cats, Suzi and Storm, jumped and chased the lights as Morven unrolled and tested them, frolicking among the pinks and blues and greens. 'Look, Ruth! Look, Linda! Firedancers!'

It was going to be a great night; it was the first party Ruth had held in many years, and in fact Morven's first ever party in all her life. She wasn't sure how to behave at parties. 'Just enjoy yourself, and make sure your guests are all enjoying themselves too,' said Aunt Ruth. 'Hand round food and drink when I ask you to, and especially look after the young folk.'

Everyone was invited to arrive at six o'clock, and soon they were all gathered. Corks were popping and soft drinks cans being ripped open, and everyone had two sticks – one for sausages and the other for marshmallows. The fire pit was a great success, keeping everyone toasty and warm and casting a warm glow around as the evening darkened.

Astrid arrived at 6:30, bringing a gift for Morven and a bottle of wine for Ruth. The gift was crayons –in a fancy box, with beautiful soft leads which left marvellously deep, vividly coloured trails, the like of which Morven had never used before. She loved them and couldn't wait to get drawing again. 'Thank you, Astrid,' she mumbled, genuinely taken aback. 'You're welcome,' said Astrid. 'I'll be looking out for your exhibitions at all the posh galleries as the years go by. Ruth, thank you so much for inviting me, it's so nice to see you both happy and settled. But I'm going to push on now,

I've got tickets for a gig in Glenbuckie, so I'll just say good-bye, and all the very best to you both.' The three of them performed a rather awkward hug, and Astrid departed for the last time. Jade slipped out to Kate's car and brought in her overnight bag. Everything was good.

As the darkness deepened, and the fire glowed brighter, several guests slipped in from the sixteenth century. Mairi and Beth and Peggy, Archie and Fiona, quietly joined the circle and were passed drinks and sausages as if they had come from the next street. Jean-Luc kept watch at the back gate. Morven hugged her special visitors and introduced them to Kyle and Jennifer and Jade. 'Family life! Mine's not so bad after all,' she reflected.

Jennifer's Dad had brought a guitar, and Jennifer her collection of drums and rattles. Some were home-made things which she had made before she even started school, and carefully preserved; others had been bought on holiday or made from junk in her Dad's shed. They sat around singing silly songs, and every time they started a new verse, they all had to swap the drums and rattles. Everyone joined in lustily. Mairi had to stop the little twins from crawling into the fire pit, and everybody helped her by picking them up and making sure they were safe, and feeding them bits of cooled toasted marshmallow. Beth and Peggy kept an eye on the sausages and handed out the newly cooked ones before they got burnt.

By the fire, the adults' conversation was turning to times long ago. Jennifer's Mum was speaking to Aunt Linda, 'You lived here long ago, didn't you Linda? I think my granny might been at school with you.'

'She's not that old!' said Kyle's Dad.

'Old enough to know where the bodies are buried!' joked Aunt Linda. 'Ruth has been doing our family tree – I think it would be safe to say that the McClures and Farriers have lived in Flegg for many generations. Maybe even many centuries.'

'So where does the name Farrier come from, then?' asked Jennifer's Mum.

'It's a blacksmith,' said Jennifer, 'didn't you know that? Farrier means blacksmith. You probably came from a family of blacksmiths from long ago in Flegg, Morven.'

Jean-Luc pricked up his ears. Morven and Mairi looked at each other, a long, understanding glance. Beth and Peggy tuned in on this; Peggy nudged Mairi. 'You know what that means, don't you?'

Mairi reached over and threw an extra log on the fire. Sparks shot up into the air, floating around, scenting the evening air with their resiny pineyness. Merlin's snicker was heard floating down by the Abbey ruins.

Jennifer's Dad picked his guitar up again. 'The answer, my friend, is blowing in the wind...'

HISTORICAL NOTE

The 16th century was a time of upheaval in Scotland, with religion and politics being turned upside down as part of the wider European Reformation movement. Mary Queen of Scots returned from France in 1661 as a young widow, having been sent there as a child. She had experienced a cultured upbringing and was already gifted in poetry and music; and she was a devout Roman Catholic. However the Reformers' plans were well advanced, and they wanted a Protestant King on the throne.

The Reformation in Scotland was led by John Knox and reprisals against Catholics were brutal. Although at times there was an uneasy truce, there were other times when Catholic sympathisers in general, and monks in particular, were captured, accused of treason, tortured, and burned at the stake.

One of the aims of the Reformers was that people should learn to read and write – principally, so that they could read the Bible and thereby be able to worship God directly instead of through the priesthood. The Bible was to be translated into English from Latin and various efforts made to raise the levels of literacy among the general population. At the beginning, women were not expected to take part in this because as a rule, they were never in positions of authority where it would be needed. Similarly, poor people and 'ordinary citizens' were not considered priority. Through time, of course, this changed.

As literacy gained greater approval, so too did the existence of the printing press. While at first, printing was seen as 'the devil's work,' it was gradually accepted as an essential tool in the service of education, both spiritual and temporal, and for the increased wellbeing of everyone.

Plague had been a recurrent problem throughout Europe for many centuries, and was still prevalent in the 16th century. There was little understanding of what caused an outbreak, and it was generally attributed to God's judgement on people for turning away from 'holy ways.' Accordingly there were calls for repentance and improved moral behaviour to cleanse the soul and body. The Plague was always more of a risk in the built-up areas of the central belt of Scotland; sometimes people would flee the cities and come to the country as a way of escaping contamination.

Pilgrimage had been a centuries-old tradition of religious life, and entailed making a long and arduous journey to a place recognised as 'holy.' St Andrews in Fife was one such place and the church there contained a 'reliquary' where the remains of saints were said to be stored. There was a well-established network of paths, inns and other services essential to the completion of the pilgrim journey. Some of these can still be traced today.

ACKNOWLEDGMENTS

Writing is rather a solitary exercise and it is a delight to get the first draft done and be able to call on others for help in slapping it into better shape. In the case of 'Hide and Speak,' I am particularly indebted to Hilary Bennison and Gillian Hogarth for detailed comments on the early drafts; Georgina McKenzie Smith for copy-editing; Donald Gilchrist for another great cover design; Claire Wingfield for typesetting and other publishing assistance; and Valerie Walker for suggesting the title. Thank you all – for your great skills and good judgement, and also for being so easy to work with.

This book was written in the first six weeks of the national Lockdown we experienced in Scotland as a result of the Covid19 pandemic. It gave me something to focus on instead of the constant bad news on TV and radio. And in that context, somewhere around the first draft of chapter 19, a nearly-member of my own family contracted the virus and was briefly very ill indeed. At that time a Thursday-night tradition was being established across the UK of showing gratitude to the National Health Service and other essential workers. Confined to our homes for most of the day, with schools, community centres, pubs, cafes, restaurants and most workplaces closed, we would emerge at 8pm with pots and pans, rattles and bells, and clap for our lives. I vividly remember being unable to participate on the first of these occasions, reduced to tears at the horrors of what might be happening right then to my future son-in-law.

Thankfully, he survived. And I returned to chapter 19 and got on with the rest of the story. And like so many others, I am learning to be grateful and patient as well as frustrated and occasionally despairing. And aware that it's so easy to forget these things. So I want to say a big thank you to all the health professionals, the carers, the shop assistants, the food producers, the delivery men and women, the volunteers, the researchers and scientists who have just got on with their jobs during this difficult time. We owe you so much.

Most of all I am grateful to friends and family for the loving contact which, as we have learned this year, keeps us all sane and ticking over. And most of all, to Dave, Harry and Kurt.

Helen Welsh was brought up in Scotland, and lives in North Fife. She has worked as a waitress, dog walker, nursing assistant, social worker, trainer, college lecturer, researcher and cook.

From an early age she wrote stories and poems, and through the years has enjoyed a range of publication and competition successes. These include, recently, stories published in Glasgow University's 'New Writing Scotland', and various other magazines and publications.

Her book 'A Life in Mouthfuls: Scottish Food and Drink Memories', was published in November 2019, and offers a lavish menu of food and drink-related stories which have been described as funny, poignant, and informative, with recipes which seem to evoke readers' own memories.

Now retired from full-time work, she works part-time as a tour guide in a local distillery. When not tour-guiding, she reads and writes, cooks, eats and drinks, participates in a community choir, and is an avid follower of the Scottish music and arts scene.

If you enjoyed this book, please help this independent author by spreading the word with a review on Amazon, Goodreads, Waterstones or any other online retailer where it is listed. If you would like guidance on how to do this, please contact Helen via her website www.hlwelsh.co.uk.

Few things are more thrilling to an author than seeing how far their stories have travelled. You can share your photos with Helen via the contact details on her website or on social media using the hashtag #LabyrinthatFlegg – thank you so much for your support.

A Life in Mouthfuls: Scottish Food and Drink Memories

Growing up in Scotland does not necessarily mean a daily diet of salmon and scallops, venison and haggis, whisky and shortbread! In this book, H L Welsh shares her food and drink memories of good times, hard times, disasters and celebrations. Along the way she includes recipes and wisdom gathered from her many mentors – elegance in simplicity; generosity even in hard times; good conversation at table; and having a bit of fun on the journey. This is not a cookbook – it's a book about eating, drinking and living well, and sharing all this with others.

The Labyrinth at Flegg is the first book in **The Flegg Trilogy**, with **Hide and Speak** being the second and the third due in Summer 2021. If you would like to know what happens next with Jean-Luc, Mairi, Josef, Morven and Ruth, sign up for notification of publication dates at www.hlwelsh.co.uk

Tales of the Auld Grey Toun is a collection of short stories set in suburban East Scotland. There is a lot of mystery, a little romance, and a surprising magical edge. Follow the adventures of Jeanie, Fairy Fay, Margaret the new-home sales advisor, Jim the bereaved single parent, Maria the pregnant teenager, and others as they dip in and out of each other's adventures.

9 781916 241848